ABOUT THE

D1396439

Michael Coleman was born in Forest Gate,
East London. In his life journey from aspiring
footballer to full-time writer he has variously been
employed as a waiter, a computer programmer,
a university lecturer, a software quality assurance
consultant and a charity worker. He is married,
with four children and one grandchild.

Michael has written many novels, including the
Carnegie Medal shortlisted *Weirdo's War*. His website
can be found at www.michael-coleman.com

The Hunting Forest is the third and final title in
The Bear Kingdom trilogy. Look out for the
first and second books, *The Howling Tower* and
The Fighting Pit.

Acclaim for *Weirdo's War*:

'Tense, psychological and instructive.' *The Times*

'As thought-provoking as it is exciting...addresses
fundamental truths about human character
and behaviour.' *Booktrusted News*

For librarians-school where-every

ORCHARD BOOKS
338 Euston Road, London NW1 3BH
Orchard Books Australia
Level 17, 207 Kent Street, Sydney, NSW 2000, Australia

ISBN: 978 1 84616 044 8

First published in 2007 by Orchard Books
A paperback original
Text © Wordjuggling Limited 2007
The right of Michael Coleman to be identified as
the author of this work has been asserted by him in
accordance with the Copyright, Designs and Patents Act, 1988.
A CIP catalogue record for this book is available from the British Library.

1 3 5 7 9 10 8 6 4 2
Printed in Great Britain

Orchard Books is a division of Hachette Children's Books

www.orchardbooks.co.uk

THE BEAR KINGDOM

THE HUNTING FOREST

MICHAEL COLEMAN

ORCHARD BOOKS

CONTENTS

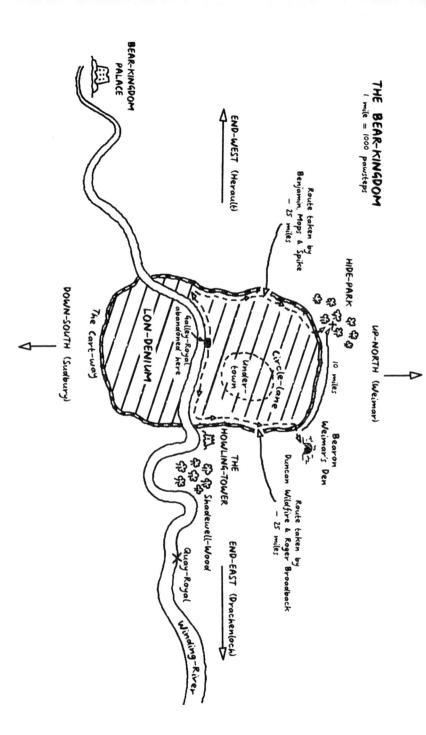

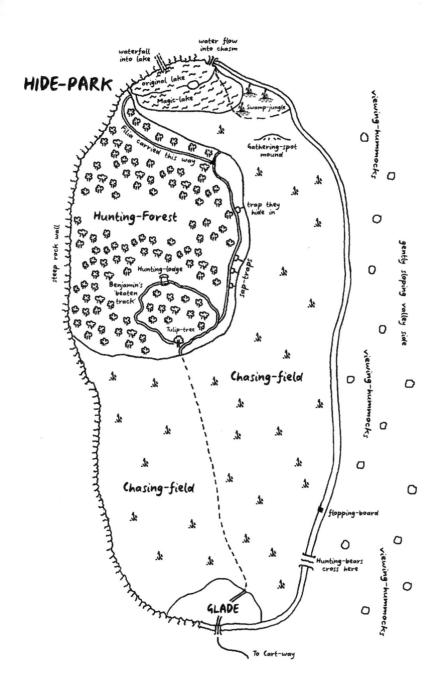

THE CART-WAY

Benjamin Wildfire and his friends, Millicent Ophelia Patience Snubnose (Mops, for short) and Spike Brownberry, turned their backs on Lon-denium's Winding-River and began their journey north. Their destination: the fabled Hide-Park of Benjamin's dreams, the one place in Bear Kingdom where humans were allowed to run free.

Behind them, the ornate Galley-Royal of King Antonius and his wife Queen Dearie, in which the three had made their escape from Bearkingdom-Palace, bobbed aimlessly up and down. Soon the tide would float it further down river and eventually out into the wild Sea-Northern. There it would be battered by waves for two sun-comes before finally sinking in a fountain of bubbles.

By then Benjamin, Mops and Spike had made surprisingly good progress. With Mops directing them from a plan-town she'd copied from one on the Galley-Royal, they'd been moving due west. Now, as she led them out from the long belt of trees they'd been following, she gave a delighted screech.

'Ta-raa!'

They'd reached a wide cart-way. To their right, it stretched away into the distance. To their left, it ran for a short way before curving out of sight.

'Is this really it?' asked Benjamin, wide-eyed, 'the big cart-way that goes all the way round the outside of Lon-denium?'

'None other,' said Mops, waggling her plan proudly. 'Turn right here, and it will lead us all the way to Hide-Park.'

'I can't believe it!' cried Benjamin happily.

'Nor me, matey,' agreed Spike, but solemnly. 'It's all too easy. I don't like it.'

Mops rolled her eyes and sighed. 'Well, that's nothing unusual is it, Spike? It could rain food and drink and you'd find a reason for not liking it.'

Spike didn't argue. He suddenly pointed along the cart-way to their left and cried, 'Danger!'

A large cart, heading north, was just rounding the bend. Frantically, Benjamin looked around for somewhere better for them to take cover than the sparse belt of trees they'd just left. Then he saw it. Just a short way off, right beside the cart-way, was an open crescent of flattened earth. The space seemed to have been cleared deliberately, for just behind it stood a dense thicket of bushes.

'Over there!' he cried.

With Mops and Spike following hard on his heels, Benjamin raced across. Within moments the three of them had dived under cover, their hearts thumping with fear. Any human – or 'sap' as the bears called them – caught without his or her bear owner was in terrible danger. Although there were rules about returning saps to their owners, almost all bears would growl 'keepers-finders!' and keep the sap they'd caught for themselves. After that, anything could happen. The poor human could be put to work, sold – or worse. The three friends had already suffered from terrible experiments in a place called the Howling-Tower, then been enslaved by King Antonius and Queen Dearie in Bearkingdom-Palace. But to have their dream of freedom in Hide-Park snatched away from them now, thought Benjamin…that would be the most awful thing of all.

Hoping desperately that they were well hidden, Benjamin peered out through the greenery to watch for when the cart passed by. But, to his horror, the cart *didn't* pass by…

It slowly pulled off the cart-way, onto the crescent of earth, and stopped. Benjamin now saw exactly what sort of cart it was – and shuddered. It was a cage-cart. Together with Mops and Spike, Benjamin had once been locked in such a cart and taken to a market. He knew just how awful the occupants of this cage-cart must be feeling. They would be cold and tired and hungry and – above all – frightened about what was going to happen to them.

Benjamin had time to see no more than that the cart held a frizzy-haired girl and a skinny boy before the driver-bear suddenly lumbered into view. As ever, when seen close-up, the bear looked huge. This one was a powerful brown bear with broad shoulders and a belly so fat that it almost scraped the ground as he moved. He'd been pulling the cart himself, using a harness looped around his shoulders. (Not a rich bear, then, reasoned Benjamin; rich bears used teams of humans to pull their carts.)

'Get ready to run if he comes our way,' Spike hissed.

'For once, I agree with you,' whispered Mops. 'I do *not* want to end up in that cage!'

But the brown bear didn't come their way. Tired from his efforts, he padded slowly to the far end of the crescent of earth and flopped to the ground. There he began to open a large package he'd been carrying.

'We must be down-wind of him,' said Benjamin, with a sigh of relief. 'He can't smell us.'

'But I can smell him,' sighed Mops. 'Or, rather, what he's got. Food!'

The aroma was mouth-watering. Hunks of baked dough dotted with berries, roots which smelled fresh enough to have been pulled up at the crack of sun-come, and – as their ears told them when the brown bear began eating – a large pile of the ripest, crunchiest apples.

Even more disturbing, though, were the pitiful cries

of hunger that had started to come from the boy and girl in the cage-cart. They were begging for something to eat. Even though the brown bear couldn't understand them (to bears, human speech usually sounds like the twittering of a flock of birds) he must have realised why the boy and girl were crying. And yet he completely ignored them.

Benjamin couldn't. When he was in Bearkingdom-Palace he'd been deliberately starved by King Antonius. He knew how awful it felt, how the gnawing emptiness in his stomach had almost been enough to drive him mad. He had to help the boy and girl in the cage-cart if he could. And so, trying not think of the danger, Benjamin slithered out from their hiding place.

By the time that Mops had hissed, 'What are you *doing*?' he was crawling on his hands and knees towards the cage-cart. Its door was secured by the flimsiest of wooden latches. If he could undo it, then the boy and girl inside would have a chance of jumping unseen to their freedom. They'd have a chance of finding some food for themselves – and the fat brown bear would arrive at his destination with an empty cage!

Benjamin crept closer. He could see that the frizzy-haired girl was about his age. The skinny boy had to be at least two summers younger. Neither of them had yet spotted him – they were too busy looking out to where the brown bear was lolling. But, suddenly, the boy swung round.

As he caught sight of Benjamin, his mouth fell open in surprise. Then, to Benjamin's horror, he squealed, 'Save us!'

Desperately, Benjamin held a finger to his lips. But the boy simply cried all the louder, 'Save us, whoever you are!'

Now the frizzy-haired girl joined in. With tears coursing down her face she screamed at the top of her voice, 'Please! Please! Please!'

'Quiet-be!' roared the brown bear, unable to ignore the children any longer, so loud had their cries become. Lumbering angrily to his feet, he began stalking towards the cage-cart.

The sight of the beast coming his way filled Benjamin with dread. One slash from those claws and he would know no more. But there was no way that he could get back to the safety of the bushes without being seen. If the bear came after him he might catch Mops and Spike as well. No, there was only one thing that Benjamin could do. Quickly, he slid under the cage-cart.

'Quiet-be, say-me!' he heard the bear roar at his two captives. In the cage-cart, the children's shouts turned to even louder wails of fear.

But now there was nothing Benjamin could do to save them – or himself, for that matter. With the wheels of the cart on each side of him, and its mud-caked floor just above his head, he was well and truly stuck. His heart was thumping with fear. All that bear would need to do to catch him was to bend down and stretch out a long-clawed paw…

Benjamin closed his eyes and waited for the pain of sharp claws digging into his flesh. It didn't come. Instead, he heard the brown bear give a roar of irritation. Flicking open his eyes again, Benjamin saw his thick legs stalking to the front of the cage-cart. Within moments, having given up all hope of the tasty meal and gentle snooze he'd stopped for, the bear had strapped himself back into his harness and was heaving the cart into motion.

Benjamin flattened himself against the ground until the cart had passed over him. Then, shakily, he got to his feet and scurried back to where Mops and Spike were still hiding fearfully. There they watched silently until the two weeping faces at the cage-cart's bars were far away.

'What you did was very brave, Benjamin,' said Mops, breaking the sad silence. 'But, if you don't mind me saying so, also very stupid.'

'I wanted to free them,' said Benjamin softly. 'I couldn't bear to think of them going hungry. I wish they could have come to Hide-Park with us.'

'That's all very well, but for a moment there it looked as though *you* wouldn't be coming to Hide-Park with *us* – isn't that right, Spike?' No answer. 'Spike? Now where is *he* going?'

Having checked that the cart-way was clear, Spike

was scurrying towards the spot where the brown bear had been about to snooze. 'Thought so,' he called as he reached it, 'that bear left behind some of his food. Hey, and there's more!'

Benjamin and Mops hurried out to join him. It was true. As well as the remains of the brown bear's meal, there were more scraps of tasty food littering the whole of the clearing.

'What's it all doing here?' asked Benjamin, his mouth full of a crunchy half-apple that he'd cleaned with his shirt sleeve.

'*That* might be part of the answer,' said Mops, pointing back to a small sign by the side of the cart-way. 'It says, "BY-LAY". Perhaps this place is where travelling bears stop and have a lie down. In which case,' she added cheerfully, 'the way to Hide-Park could be absolutely *littered* with food!'

Mops was right. As they walked on they regularly came to by-lays – and found food that had been carelessly tossed away every time. So it was that, over the course of the next eleven sun-comes (Benjamin counted them), they didn't go hungry.

Fortunately they didn't have any more scares. It helped that for much of the time, they were careful to stay hidden – especially just after sun-come and just before sun-go, when it seemed there was a constant stream of carts rattling by. During other periods of the light-time, though, the cart-way had been quiet. Then they'd seize the chance to creep out and journey on as quickly as they could.

They'd made good progress. At least, that was what Mops was insisting. She was studying her little plan-town more and more often – sometimes with a nod and sometimes with a frown.

'Are we nearly there yet?' Spike had asked more than once, only to be told to stop worrying and keep walking.

Now, as they drew near to a point where a narrower cart-track crossed the cart-way, Mops halted. For here, just as there'd been at similar spots along the way, an upright wooden post had been planted in the earth.

'They're called post-signs,' Mops had said each time, glancing up at it then walking on. But this time she'd stopped and looked closer. Benjamin knew from the way that she was studying it that this one was different.

Sticking out from the sign at right angles were four pieces of wood, each shaped like a pointing claw. Two were pointing to the sides, in the direction of the crossing track. One claw was pointing back the way they'd come. As for the fourth – that was pointing straight ahead, the way they were going. Each of the pointing claws had some writing on.

'That's a relief,' breathed Mops. 'Not that I had any doubts, of course.'

'Well, what does it *say*?' asked Benjamin impatiently.

'It says,' Mops announced proudly, '"Up-North.

1000"'. She looked at Benjamin and laughed delightedly. 'Hear that? Only one thousand paw-paces to Bearon Weimar's quarter of Bear-Kingdom.'

Spike shuddered. 'Just so long as we don't run into him,' he said grimly.

Neither Benjamin nor Mops could deny that Spike had a right to be gloomy where Bearon Weimar was concerned. After his escape from the Howling-Tower, Spike had unluckily fallen into Bearon Weimar's clutches. It was he who'd forced Spike into becoming a fighting-sap, putting him up against other boys (such as Benjamin!) and betting that Spike would beat them – but only after both fighters had shed plenty of blood.

'We won't meet any bears in Hide-Park,' said Benjamin confidently. 'It'll just be us, as free as the air.'

'Sounds too good to be true,' replied Spike. 'It wouldn't surprise me if the place doesn't exist at *all*.'

'Oh, Spike!' cried Benjamin. 'Of course it does! Didn't we hear that family at Fleeceham Market say they'd been there? And Mops saw it on the Galley-Master's plan-town! What more proof do you need?'

'How about a post-sign?' said Mops suddenly.

She was still looking up at the pointer showing that they were heading towards the Up-North region controlled by Bearon Weimar. But now Benjamin noticed that beneath it another, smaller pointer was swinging from a pair of rusty hooks. It was this smaller pointer that Mops was referring to.

'What does it say?' asked Benjamin.

'It says, "Hide-Park. 1500."'

'What!' cried Benjamin in delight.

He punched the air. He hugged Mops. He danced a little jig with an astonished Spike. They were just one thousand five hundred paw-paces from Hide-Park! One sun-come's worth of cautious walking, two at the most. Then they would be there, running free. It would be everything that his father's stories had promised, he knew it would. No chains, no fear – just the happiness that came from being free. It was going to be all he'd ever dreamed of.

No, that wasn't true. *Almost* all. To make his dream complete, his father and mother would need to be there too. As he, Mops and Spike ended their celebrations and resumed their journey, Benjamin wondered – as he had so many times since they'd parted – whether his father was safe...

JOURNEY'S END

Duncan Wildfire's journey had, so far, been uneventful. He and his companion, Roger Broadback (saved with him by Benjamin, Mops and Spike from the dreadful life of a galley-sap on the Galley-Royal) had, of course, moved very carefully.

The first part of their route had taken them along the banks of the Winding-River which cut through the centre of Lon-denium. There the tall reeds and rushes provided plenty of cover. After six sun-comes' travelling they, like Benjamin and his friends, had reached the cart-way which circled the capital of Bear Kingdom. In their case, of course, it was the part of the cart-way that ran along the east side of Lon-denium. It was as they reached a wooden board by the side of the cart-way that Duncan's heart was suddenly chilled by a terrible fear.

They were using a small plan-town that Mops had drawn for them on a square of rough parchment. Duncan had been amazed to discover that during her time in Bearkingdom-Palace, Benjamin's friend had learned how to write. Neither he nor Roger could even read. Mops had carefully written two bear-words on the plan for them to look out for, though. The first of these words was:

END-EAST

Bear Kingdom was divided into four quarters, each controlled on behalf of the king and queen by one of four bearons: End-West by Bearon Herault, End-East by Bearon Drachenloch, Down-South by Bearon Sudbury and Up-North by Bearon Weimar. The sign-board they'd reached could mean only one thing – they were crossing into End-East, the region of Bear Kingdom controlled by Bearon Drachenloch. And that meant into the region which contained the terrible Howling-Tower, where he and his wife Alicia had once been held captive.

Trying to close his mind to the horrors he'd experienced in that place, Duncan hurried Roger along the cart-way as quickly as he could. Although both fully grown humans, they were only moving at much the same speed as the younger Benjamin, Mops and Spike had been. Duncan, in particular, had been weakened so much by his time as a galley-sap on the Galley-Royal that he needed to rest often.

With every step they took, Duncan's weary eyes now began to search for a second board – one displaying the other bear-word that Mops had written down for them…

Finally, after five more sun-comes' walking, they came to the end of a long curving bend. And there it was:

UP-NORTH

Hope replaced anxiety in Duncan Wildfire's heart. He felt as if some of his strength was returning.

The sign meant they had left Bearon Drachenloch's region and were passing into that of Bearon Weimar. More importantly, they were getting closer to Bearon Weimar's den – which meant they were getting closer to his wife, and Benjamin's mother, Alicia. If what his son had discovered was true, that's where she was. The sheer thought of his dear wife being won by Bearon Weimar in a bet brought tears to his eyes. As for her being forced to spend her days standing totally still on a pedestal as a beautiful stone-painted never-move, Duncan couldn't imagine anything more pointless and cruel. He would rescue her from that torture if it was the last thing he did.

After passing the UP-NORTH sign, Roger Broadback strode ahead with Mops' miniature plan-town in his hand. Duncan followed behind, keeping a sharp look-out for danger.

'How do we know how far it is?' called Roger over his shoulder. He was panting, for the cart-way was taking them up quite a steep incline.

'We don't,' said Duncan. 'Just that it's somewhere off to the right of this cart-way.'

'Which means it may be hidden behind some of this lot,' said Roger solemnly, waving the plan-town at the thickly-growing trees towering on either side of them. 'We could easily miss it.'

'I don't think so,' replied Duncan. 'Spike told me that Bearon Weimar's den is big...'

'Helpful,' smiled Roger.

'But, much more importantly, that there is a portrait of the Bearon claw-cut into the roof. Now what does that tell you?'

'That he loves himself?'

'True,' called Duncan Wildfire, falling a little way behind as the incline got steeper. 'Most important bears do. But I doubt if that's why he's had that picture done. No, when you're important, you want everybody *else* to know it. I'm hoping that's why he's had it carved into his den's roof – so that it can be seen from a long way away...'

Ahead, Roger Broadback had stopped in admiration. He turned, waiting for Duncan to catch him up. Then he said, 'I can see where Benjamin gets his brains from.'

They'd reached the top of the incline. There, the cart-way curved gently to the left as it sloped downhill. To its right, but straight ahead as they looked, lay a wide and thickly-wooded valley. At its centre was a sprawling and important-looking den. Carved in its sloping, wooden roof, and impossible to miss, was a portrait.

It showed a bear sideways on – a bear with silvery-grey fur and a muzzle of white. His eye glinted glassily in the sun, making him look both fierce and cunning.

'Bearon Weimar's den,' breathed Duncan.

Roger nodded. 'Now you can keep your promise to your son, and rescue his mother.'

Duncan felt elated at the thought. He briefly wondered, as he had time and again throughout their journey, how Benjamin and his two friends were getting on in their quest to reach Hide-Park. Then he set his mind back to thinking about how were they going to break in to Bearon Weimar's den.

At that moment, on the other side of the cart-way, Benjamin was feeling as elated as his father. Ever since the '1500' post-sign, their progress towards Hide-Park had been regularly marked...two further post-signs had said it was first one thousand, then seven hundred and fifty paw-paces away. Now the three of them were staring up at a post-sign which read (according to Mops):

HIDE-PARK, 500

It was no longer pointing straight on, though. Instead, it was directing them towards a wide and well-beaten track which led off from the main cart-way and up towards the brow of a steep hill.

'Does your plan-town say it's this way?' Benjamin asked Mops.

'Roughly,' replied Mops.

'What's that supposed to mean, Squawker?' said Spike. 'Is this the right way or not?'

Mops raised her hands and shook her head at the same time. 'I'm sorry, but this is not an exact drawing. 'Roughly' is the best I can say. Why don't we just go up to the top of the hill and see?'

Benjamin led the way along the track, full of nervous hope. He was concentrating so hard on reaching the top that he didn't even hear Spike wondering aloud, 'Why's this track so wide?' or 'And why's it so worn?'

It was left to Mops to answer, 'Who cares what it looks like, as long as it's going the right way!'

They were nearly there. As the trees and bushes flanking the track grew thicker, Benjamin felt confident enough about not being spotted that he allowed himself to break into a run. His heart was pounding. What would Hide-Park be like? Would it be as glorious a place as his father's stories had led him to believe? Desperately, anxiously, he scrambled up the last few paces to the brow of the hill. There, all he could do was stand and stare.

'Oh, Benjamin!' gasped Mops as she reached his side.

Spike arrived at his other side. 'Look at that,' was all he could manage.

Down beneath them, nestling in the hollow of a huge valley, was a large space. At the far end was a vast lake, twinkling and blue. Through its centre ran a forest of towering trees, their leaves golden in the sunlight. To the sides of this forest were wide, open grassy spaces.

And on those spaces, Benjamin could just make out small figures. Two-legged figures. Humans, like them. Some were running. Others were skipping. Yet more were jumping. And all were free. Not a bear was in sight.

His father's stories about Hide-Park were true, all true!

'We've found it,' he sighed.

But finding Hide-Park was only a start. If his dreams were to come true, more action was needed. And so, just like Duncan Wildfire when he'd seen Bearon Weimar's den, Benjamin now set his mind to thinking about how they were going to get in.

THE CHASM AND THE BRIDGE

Feeling suddenly nervous about being out in the open at the top of the hill, Benjamin cautiously suggested that they lie low until they worked out what their next move should be. 'After getting this far, the last thing we want to do is get caught,' he said.

Spike nodded. 'There could be traps we can't see.'

Mops, though, pointed at the running and playing figures in the distance. 'Well they've all managed to get in, so it can't be that difficult, can it? *I* suggest we get a bit nearer.'

'I agree with Benjamin. I think we should wait for a bit.'

'Outvoted,' sighed Mops. 'Very well.'

So they retreated into a patch of low, scrubby bushes to survey Hide-Park and its surroundings in more detail.

'It looks like that side isn't going to have a way in,' said Benjamin, with a wide sweep of his left arm.

The natural bowl in which the valley sat wasn't same all the way round. The whole of the left-hand side was a steep wall of rock, sprinkled with hardy green bushes and tumbling plants. It rose from the floor of the valley down below, ended high above them, and extended halfway round behind the twinkling lake in the distance.

Benjamin turned his attention to the right-hand side of the valley. This looked far more hopeful. There the land sloped gently down to the valley floor. But his hopes that it might provide a way in were quickly dashed by Spike.

'And I don't see how we're going to get over *that*,' he pointed.

For at the bottom of the slope, and running the whole length of the right side of the valley, was what looked like a long, winding crack in the earth. Looking down on it as they were, it was hard to tell quite how wide it was, or how deep – only that to get in to Hide-Park from that side would mean getting across it somehow.

Mops sighed. 'Forgive me if I'm being Miss Obvious here…but isn't the way in likely to be at the end of the track which brought us up here from the cart-way? If we follow it a bit further and get a bit nearer – as I suggested some while ago – it could put a stop to all this guessing.'

'There could be guard-bears,' said Benjamin cautiously.

'Patrolling,' nodded Spike.

Mops sighed yet again. 'Benjamin. Spike. We have been in the Howling-Tower. We have been in Bearkingdom-Palace. Each of them had guard-bears by the bucketful – and did we have any trouble spotting them? No. They made themselves very visible indeed. Now, tell me: can you see any bears down below?'

Benjamin and Spike shook their heads. In the centre of Hide-Park, where the humans were running and jumping, not a bear could be seen. The same was true for the gentle slopes on the right side of the valley, and even the steep rocky wall on their left (which a sure-pawed bear could probably have scaled); both were bear-free.

'So, unless there's a whole gang of them lying in wait at the end of the track,' Mops continued, 'Hide-Park does appear to be a bear-free zone.' She smiled delightedly. 'In other words, Benjamin, it seems as if your father's stories about Hide-Park are *true!*'

Benjamin was convinced. He grinned from ear to ear. Even Spike gave a nod and frowned less deeply. And so they made their way back to the track and began to head along it. Unsurprisingly, it led downwards. For a while they could see the valley clearly. Then, as the track led them into a belt of tall trees, it disappeared from view. On they went, down and down, their hopes bubbling – until finally they were bursting out into the open again to get their first real look at the nearest part of the valley floor – that part that had been hidden from them when they were higher up.

'We *have* got to go across that – that – whatever it is!' cried Mops.

'Chasm,' said Spike gloomily.

Benjamin's heart sank. The deep crack in the earth didn't only run the whole length of the right-hand side of Hide-Park. As they could now see, it also curved round and stretched across the front as well. It only ended at the point where it met the rock wall. There it dipped sharply, heading beneath the rock to some subterranean destination, like a snake slithering silently towards its lair.

They continued walking, but now in subdued silence. The chasm had to be at least five paw-paces wide, estimated Benjamin, and even wider than that in some places. As for how deep it was, that they would only be able to tell when they got closer and looked over the edge...

A sudden growl-laugh, coming from back along the track, swept all these thoughts from Benjamin's mind.

'Bears!' he said urgently. 'Take cover!'

'Where?' cried Mops.

Without realising it, the three of them had walked a good twenty paw-paces away from where the track emerged from the belt of trees. Were they to run back now, they would be in danger of meeting the bear coming the other way.

'There!' urged Spike, pointing.

There was a low grassy hummock, not much taller than themselves, away to their left. It would have to do.

The three friends raced across to it and slithered to

the ground behind it. They were just in time. Another growl-laugh carried their way, far closer this time. Then a command, 'Patient-be!' followed by another from a second bear, 'Nearly-you-there!'

The sound of the two bears' paws scratching over the hard earth of the track grew, peaked and began to fade – a sure sign that they were heading on down to the valley floor, close to the chasm. Flat on his front, Benjamin slithered round the bottom of the hummock. Spike and Mops followed. There they discovered to their relief and delight that their new hiding spot couldn't have been better. They could see right down to the valley floor itself, no more than fifty paw-paces away. More importantly, they could clearly see the two bears.

They were both carrying sacks over their humped shoulders – sacks which were wriggling and twisting! Down the track the two bears lumbered, until they reached a point where it expanded into a wide bare circle. There they lowered their sacks…and tipped them upside down.

'Humans!' gasped Benjamin.

Out of each sack tumbled a mixture of arms and legs which quickly rearranged themselves and scrambled to their feet. One was a frizzy-haired girl, the other a skinny-legged boy. They looked familiar. *More* than familiar.

'They're the two from the cage-cart, matey!'

said Spike. 'The ones you tried to rescue!'

Spike was right. How they'd arrived here before the boy and girl was a mystery. So too was the fact that neither of the sack-carrying bears was the fat-bellied brown bear who'd stopped his cage-cart at the by-lay. But here the two captive children certainly were. The boy was looking around, dazed, clearly wondering where he was. Then the frizzy-haired girl caught sight of the chasm close by. She let out a scream of panic.

'Oh, no!' cried Mops. 'They're not going to push them down there...'

She began to scramble to her feet, ready to attract the bears' attention, but Benjamin grabbed hold of her by the shoulders and pulled her back – for it looked to him as though the children weren't in any danger. True, both bears had their paws stretched wide, but not so as to grab the children. They were trying to usher them...but to where?

Benjamin couldn't see. Another hummock – there were lines of them dotted around this side of the valley, he noticed – was in the way. Quickly he scrambled down to it on all fours, again with Spike and Mops in pursuit. But this time, instead of peering round the side of the hummock, the three friends climbed up to peer cautiously over its top.

And there they discovered the answer to the question of how to get in to Hide-Park.

Tucked away in a hollow on the floor of the valley

was a narrow bridge. It was made of three thick, claw-felled tree trunks which had been laid across the chasm and lashed together at both ends with strong vines.

It was this bridge that the two bears seemed to be ushering the boy and girl towards. But the two frightened children didn't want to move. All they could see when they glanced over their shoulders was the yawning chasm. When they finally saw the bridge they looked at it in amazement. And when the bears pointed across to the other side, they were so stunned they stopped crying.

'They...they're sending them across!' gasped Mops as she saw the scene unfolding below them.

The frizzy-haired girl was stepping hesitantly onto the bridge. Encouraged by this, the boy joined her. Still looking as if they couldn't believe what was happening, they stopped and stood stock still. Only when one of the bears, with a distinctive grey patch of fur in the centre of his otherwise brown chest, waved his forepaws and shouted 'over-go!' did it finally seem to sink in.

Slowly the two children began to edge across the bridge. One step, two steps...until, as they saw that the bears weren't following them, they began to race joyfully the rest of the way over. Moments later they'd plunged through the ranks of trees which bordered the other side of the chasm and disappeared from view.

'It's...as easy as *that*?' murmured Mops. 'You just *walk* in?'

Benjamin was lost for words. It certainly looked that way. Below, the two bears had already slung their empty sacks over their shoulders and were starting to pad cheerfully back up the track. Sliding down the hummock, Benjamin, Mops and Spike hid in silence until the bears had vanished from view.

Only then did Benjamin say, 'It looks like you *do* just walk in, Mops.' His face broke into a huge smile. 'Hide-Park really is as free as that!'

'I don't like it,' muttered Spike.

Benjamin sighed. He knew Spike was cautious, but he was also a true and brave friend. So his opinion mattered. '*Why* don't you like it?' he asked.

Spike merely shrugged. 'I don't know why. I just don't. I mean, how come those children were brought here? Why weren't they sold or…' Spike shuddered, as he remembered what a previous owner had done to him, '…just chucked in some river?'

'Perhaps because, after buying them from that cage-cart-puller,' said Mops, 'those bears took pity on them and brought them here?'

'They were being kind-hearted, you mean?' said Spike suspiciously.

Mops frowned. 'I suppose I do.'

'Right,' said Spike. 'And have you ever known a kind-hearted bear, Squawker? 'Cos I haven't.'

Spike had a point, realised Benjamin. But, if

they weren't simply being kind-hearted, why else would those two bears have brought those children here and set them free? He had to know.

'I'm going down there,' Benjamin said suddenly.

'No, matey,' urged Spike. 'You don't know what'll happen.'

But Benjamin was already clambering to his feet. 'Then there's only one way to find out,' he said. 'You two keep watch. If there's any danger, whistle.'

He moved quickly. In next to no time he was at the foot of the bridge. He scanned the bank of trees on the other side for any sign of a guard-bear. He saw none. He looked to his left and right. Again, Benjamin didn't see the slightest hint of any danger. So he started to cross the tree-trunk bridge.

As he moved, Benjamin couldn't help looking down into the chasm. Its sheer sides plummeted down to a bed of jagged rocks. Trickling around these rocks was a thin course of muddy water. The drop looked maybe fifteen or twenty paces deep, Benjamin couldn't be sure. What he was sure about, though, was that anybody unlucky enough to fall into the chasm would break every bone in their body.

Thankful for the solid trunks beneath his feet, Benjamin kept going – until, with a surge of joy, he was leaping from the end of the bridge on to the springy, needle-covered earth on the other side of the chasm. He could scarcely believe it. He'd spent his whole life dreaming of this moment and now it had arrived. He was in Hide-Park!

'Come on!' he turned and shouted up at Mops and Spike.

As they scurried down towards him, Benjamin looked for signs that they were being watched. But all he saw was the towering rock wall stretching away to his right and the green, hummock-dotted valley side reaching round to his left.

Arriving at the other side of the bridge, Mops and Spike hesitated until Benjamin repeated, 'Come on!'

Mops then led the way, keeping warily to the middle of the three tree-trunks even though the narrow gaps between them had been filled with chippings. Spike followed her, slowly and nervously, gulping whenever he glanced down into chasm. Finally, all three of them were together.

'Ready?' said Benjamin.

Mops nodded vigorously. Spike gave a sort of half-nod, half-shrug.

Benjamin turned. Ahead was a winding tunnel of gold-leafed acorn-trees. What delights would they find at the other end? Benjamin couldn't wait to find out.

Boldly and freely he strode forward, into Hide-Park...

HIDE-PARK

The floor of the tree-tunnel was soft and springy with fallen leaves. More fluttered down as they passed by, twisting and turning in the cool air. On both sides, the sturdy acorn-trees had a thick undergrowth of nut-bushes and berry-brambles.

Most of this was lost on Benjamin. His gaze was fixed straight ahead, from where he could now hear the faint sound of laughter. He hurried them on. Faster, faster. The tree-tunnel curved. He could see its end! It looked like a glowing circle of soft light. Beyond it lay an open glade. Benjamin couldn't get to it quickly enough.

They burst out from the trees into the most glorious spot they'd ever seen. The glade was wide and grassy. In the centre a group of laughing children were playing a game of cone-catch. Around the outside nestled cosy-looking log cabins. From behind one of them a wispy curl of sweet-smelling smoke was rising.

'Oh, Benjamin,' sighed Mops. 'It's heavenly!' She turned to Spike. 'I *dare* you to say you don't like *this*!'

Spike smiled sheepishly. 'I'm not going to. It's – well, great!' And he laughed.

At that moment a powerful-looking boy, perhaps two or three summers older than Benjamin, came out from a cabin nearby. He hurried over to them at once.

'I'm Armstrong,' he said. 'Who are you?'

'I'm Benjamin Wildfire,' said Benjamin. 'This is Spike Brownberry, and this is Mops.'

'Short for Millicent Ophelia Patience Snubnose,' said Mops. 'Do *you* have any more names?'

The boy shook his head. 'Only "Armstrong".'

Mops laughed happily. 'Only? What a peculiar name! Still, there you go. So – how long have you been here, Only?'

'Coming up to four moons,' said Armstrong, with a touch of pride. 'Longer than anyone here.' He pointed across the glade at a slim girl swinging on the branch of a tree. 'Mary Graceful came next. Then it was...' he pointed at a rather round grown-older woman who was standing, her chubby arms folded, watching the cone-catch game, '...that lady. Her name's Belinda Dumpling. Then it was...oh, I forget now. There's too many of us to remember.'

'How many are there?' asked Benjamin.

'Fifty, maybe. Nearer sixty now you three have turned up. Come from Bearon Weimar's as well, have you?'

Standing beside Benjamin, Spike gave a start of shock at hearing the name of the sinister bearon in charge of the Up-North region, and in whose den he'd once been held captive. 'B-Bearon Weimar's?' he said. 'What makes you ask that?'

Armstrong shrugged. 'Just that lots of the saps here have. Like the pair who got here just before you three. Come on, you can go in the cabin next door to them.'

They followed Armstrong across the dappled glade and in through the doorway of a neat log cabin. Inside, there were proper wooden bunks to sleep on and straw-filled covers to snuggle beneath. The cabin even had a small table with a collection of food bowls and drinking cups laid out on it.

'My word, Only,' said Mops, picking up a bowl and cup. 'Is our food and drink supplied as well?'

'Ignore her,' growled Spike.

'Stop teasing, Mops,' said Benjamin. 'You know we'll have to go out and find food for ourselves.'

'No, you won't,' said Armstrong. 'Well, no further than the food hoppers and water barrels down at the end of the cabins.'

Spike's mouth fell open in astonishment. 'You mean we *do* get given our food and drink?'

Armstrong nodded. 'Yep. And lots of it.'

'But how?' asked Benjamin, equally amazed.

'And who supplies it?' said Mops, adding, 'not that I particularly care, just so long as it's a regular occurrence.'

'It is,' said Armstrong. 'Every other sun-come we

wake up to find the hoppers and barrels filled to the brim again. But don't ask me how it gets here.'

The feelings of astonishment only increased when Armstrong took them across the glade to show them the food hoppers. They were great, round containers made of nut-wood. Each had a small shutter at its front. All they had to do was put their food bowl beneath the container and lift the shutter until the bowl was full.

And *what* delights those bowls were filled with! The crunchiest nuts, the sweetest fruits, the most succulent berries...

'Look at that lot, Oliver!' said an excited voice behind them. 'Best thing that happened, us getting bought by Bearon Weimar, wasn't it?'

Benjamin, Mops and Spike all swung round at the same time. Behind them stood the frizzy-haired girl and the skinny-legged boy they'd seen in the cage-cart on the way to Hide-Park. Benjamin was confused by what he'd just heard. Even so, he still apologised, 'I'm sorry I failed to set you free.'

'We're not!' said the girl.

'We were at the time,' said the boy. 'But we're not now!'

Everyone introduced themselves, then Benjamin told Armstrong how they'd seen the boy and girl tipped out of their sacks and ushered across the bridge.

'You looked surprised,' said Mops to the girl.

'Nothing new,' replied the girl, who'd said her name was Penelope Curls. 'It's been one surprise after another lately. The first was our owner-bear – the one you saw pulling the cage-cart we were in – taking us to that posh bearon.'

'Second surprise was him buying us,' piped up the boy, who'd introduced himself as Oliver Spindle. 'Our owner had tried to sell us to lots of other bears and they'd all told him they were interested-not.'

That could explain why he, Spike and Mops had reached Hide-Park before them, realised Benjamin. Penelope and Oliver's owner had been roaming round trying to sell them.

'Third surprise was to hear Bearon Weimar telling his helper-bears to give us a good meal and a comfy straw bed,' continued Penelope.

'Fourth surprise was getting shoved into those sacks,' said Oliver with a shudder. 'I didn't like that one.'

'Nor me,' continued Penelope. 'I was expecting the next stop to be the river. But what happens? Surprise, surprise, we find ourselves being shooed into this place!'

Benjamin hadn't even begun to eat from his brimming bowl. Having heard their story, he was now bursting with questions he had to ask Penelope and Oliver first.

'When you were on the way to Bearon Weimar's,' he said, his heart pounding, 'did you see a man with red hair, like mine? He would have been with another man. They could have been walking along the cart-way or hiding near Bearon Weimar's den or – anything.'

Benjamin hurried on, the words falling out in a hopeful torrent. 'Or, when you got there, did you see a beautiful never-move? She would have had red hair too. Did you? Did you?'

Penelope and Oliver both shook their heads. 'No. Sorry.'

Blinking back tears of sadness, Benjamin trudged back to his cabin and sat down to his meal. Spike and Mops joined him. By the time Benjamin's friends had finished eating, the sun was sinking low behind the trees and casting long shadows across the glade.

'Well, I have to say that was *delicious*!' said Mops.

Seeing that Benjamin had hardly touched his own food, she leaned down to put her face close to his. 'Thank you for everything, Benjamin Wildfire. And don't worry about your parents. From what I've seen of your father I fully expect him to find your mother in double-quick time. They'll probably arrive any sun-come now…and when they do they won't want to find a skinny misery of a son. So buck up!'

Benjamin grinned. Mops was right. There was a lot to be thankful for. If anybody could set his mother free from Bearon Weimar's den, his father could. And, after what Penelope and Oliver said, perhaps the bearon hadn't been treating her so cruelly after all.

'Besides,' added Mops, jerking a thumb in Spike's direction. 'One misery around the place is quite enough.'

'I am *not* miserable!' retorted Spike. 'I'm just – wondering.'

'Wondering what?' asked Benjamin.

'How come all the food and everything gets in here?' asked Spike.

'Does it matter?' cried Mops. She pointed at her rather round stomach. 'I'm more concerned about how I'm going to get it all in here!'

Spike sighed. 'Maybe you're right, Squawker. But I've said it before and I'll say it again. I've never known a kind-hearted bear.'

Benjamin awoke suddenly. His shoulder was being shaken by a strong hand. Opening his eyes he saw a shady outline, framed against the pale light coming into the cabin from outside. Spike's outline.

'What is it?' murmured Benjamin.

Spike didn't reply, just beckoned with his crooked finger. Benjamin slid out from beneath his straw-filled cover and on to the wooden floor. Silently, Spike guided him across to the window.

Swaying torch-lights were heading through the trees towards them. That they were coming from the direction of the bridge across the chasm, Benjamin had no doubt. Slowly they drew nearer, until the first broke into the glade. For one moment a terrible memory returned to haunt Benjamin – of their time in the Howling-Tower, and of the nightly inspections conducted by the evil bear in charge of that place, Inspector Dictatum. His heart began pounding, faster and faster, until the leading bear came far enough into the glade for Benjamin to make out the strange grey patch of fur in the centre of his chest.

'It's the same bear who brought Penelope and Oliver!' hissed Benjamin. A thought struck him. 'Maybe he's brought some other children.'

'At middle-night?' said Spike suspiciously.

Benjamin felt chill with fear. As more bears began crowding quietly into the glade it was clear that the bear party had brought *something* with them. They came in pairs, with each bear supporting one end of a stout pole on his broad shoulders. Swinging back and forth in the centre of each of these poles were large, bulging – but not wriggling – sacks. Other pairs of bears were struggling under the weight of dripping acorn-wood barrels.

'If they haven't brought children,' muttered Benjamin, 'what *have* they brought?'

'We'd better wake Squawker,' said Spike urgently. 'If they come this way we'll have to run fast.'

'Wait!' hissed Benjamin.

Outside, the bears were sliding their sacks and barrels silently from their carrying poles. The sacks were being lifted and their contents tipped into the food hoppers. The water barrels were being pushed into position and the empty ones loaded back onto the carrying poles.

'They might still come for us!' hissed Spike. 'I don't trust 'em...'

But the bear with the grey patch was showing no sign of coming any closer to the cabins. Quite the opposite. He was beckoning, his curved claws signalling that it was time to be moving. Two by two, they began to leave the glade. As they went, the bear with the grey patch did no more than glance across to the row of cabins with a smile. Then he followed the others through the trees, his torch-light swinging and fading until its light had vanished completely. The bears had left as quietly as they'd come.

'What *are* you two doing?' came a bleary-voiced demand from the bunk in the corner. 'What's going on?'

'Nothing, Squawker,' said Spike quietly. 'Go back to sleep.'

'Everything's fine, Mops,' murmured Benjamin.

Spike nodded and smiled. 'You were right, matey. I was wrong. It looks like this place is everything you said it would be. Kind-hearted bears *do* exist.'

'Well, hooray for that,' said Mops, snuggling back beneath her covers. 'And what's brought about this change of heart?'

'We've just seen some bears bringing fresh food and water, Mops,' said Benjamin. 'They must really care for us.'

Spike climbed back onto his own bunk. 'That bear with the grey patch was in charge. The one who brought Penelope and Oliver from Bearon Weimar's.'

Spike paused, as the real meaning of what he was saying sank in. 'Then...it's Bearon Weimar who's giving us all this?'

'Obviously,' said Mops. 'Which can mean only one thing, of course. Chancellor Bruno and the four bearons must have won the battle of Bearkingdom-Palace. If not, King Antonius and Queen Dearie would have punished them for sure. Bearon Weimar would have been searching for his head, not giving us food and freedom in Hide-Park...' Her voice tailed off as she realised exactly what she was saying.

It was Benjamin who put it into words. 'It doesn't make sense, does it?'

'If you're thinking what I'm thinking, Benjamin,' said Mops, 'then – no, it doesn't.'

'Bearon Weimar *doesn't* care for saps,' said Spike. 'He turned me into a fighter and put bets on me.'

'He tried to have me as a never-move,' said Mops, fiercely.

Benjamin forced the words out. 'He won my mother from King Antonius in a bet and uses *her* as a never-move.'

Could it be that the same bear could be both cruel and kind? It just didn't seem possible.

'Maybe he's had a change of heart,' said Mops when Benjamin voiced his fears. 'Perhaps being one of the Bear Kingdom's rulers has made him more of a care-bear.'

'No chance, Squawker,' growled Spike.

They talked about it for a little longer and agreed

there was nothing they could do there and now. Perhaps in the following sun-comes they would find out more. Finally Spike and Mops fell asleep.

But Benjamin lay awake, thinking. Could Bearon Weimar really have changed from being cruel enough to make Spike into a fighting-sap to being so kind that he'd save children and keep them well fed? If so, perhaps his father wouldn't have to rescue his mother at all; perhaps she would have already been set free. But if he was still as cruel as before...

Benjamin shuddered. When finally his eyes closed, his mind was still trying to block out the thought of what dangers might face his father and Roger Broadback when they finally reached Bearon Weimar's den.

BEARON WEIMAR AND
HIS VISITOR

After spotting Bearon Weimar's den, with its portrait of the Bearon himself carved into its roof, Duncan Wildfire and Roger Broadback had proceeded with great care. Knowing how well guarded such an important den was likely to be, they'd approached it by a roundabout route. After leaving the cart-way, they'd weaved their way slowly through the trees and down towards the den. Every so often, Roger had cut a small notch from the bark of a tree so that they'd be able to find their way back again quickly.

'We might be lucky,' Duncan Wildfire had told him. 'If my Alicia is outside in the grounds of Weimar's den, then we might be able to set her free quite easily.'

But that hadn't proved to be the case. They'd reached the clearing surrounding Bearon Weimar's den without any difficulty. Once there, Duncan had left Roger watching for any movement in and out of the den itself while he'd set about creeping the length and breadth of the Bearon's grounds. Alicia was nowhere to be seen. Grim-faced, Duncan had returned (at about the same time that Benjamin, Mops and Spike were crossing the bridge into Hide-Park) to where Roger lay hidden in the depths of a sprawling clump of nut-bushes.

'Alicia *must* be inside the den,' he said. 'Have you seen anything?'

Roger shook his head. 'No humans. But a big bear turned up at the door and went in a little while ago.'

Duncan gazed across from their hiding place towards the huge wooden door which formed the entrance to Bearon Weimar's den. 'Did you manage to see anything when the door opened? What was inside?'

Again, Roger shook his head. 'Sorry. The visiting bear just about filled the doorway.'

Duncan looked again at Bearon Weimar's door and frowned. 'He *must* have been big, then.'

'He was,' said Roger with a shudder. 'Probably the biggest bear I've ever seen.'

Bearon Weimar's entertaining-chamber was spacious and comfortable. Rays of sunlight flooded down into the room from the square window in the roof, warming the soft reeds and rushes covering the floor. Claw-drawn portraits of the bearon and his fore-bears were etched into the pale walls. And, to complete the setting, standing on her pedestal in a purpose-built alcove, was the most beautiful red-haired never-move. Her name: Alicia Wildfire.

As usual Benjamin's mother had been woken, had her

skin painted the colour of stone, been dressed in a stone-coloured garment, had her lustrous red hair brushed out over her slim shoulders, then been brought to the chamber to have her feet manacled to her square pedestal. Not for an instant had there been a chance to escape. On or off her pedestal, she'd always been under lock and key. All she'd ever been able to do was stand and look beautiful for her owners – first the king and queen, and now Bearon Weimar. But though they owned her body, they couldn't own her mind. So Alicia Wildfire had spent every moment of her existence thinking of her son Benjamin and her husband Duncan – every moment, that is, until now. Now her mind was being taken over by such fearful memories that it was all Alicia Wildfire could do to stop herself trembling from head to toe.

It was the bear sitting bolt upright in the middle of the entertaining-chamber floor that was frightening her. His eyes were still as piercing as she remembered them, his claws still the longest and sharpest she'd ever seen. And he was still the biggest bear she'd ever seen too – so big that his shadow was reached from the middle of the floor to partly cover her. It was this bear who now spoke.

'Congratulations-many, Bearon Weimar. Bear Kingdom place-better without King Antonius and Queen Dearie.'

The silvery-grey bear lounging opposite inclined his head and raised a four-clawed paw in acknowledgement.

His pure white muzzle creased into a smile. 'Chancellor Bruno King-become soon-very.'

Alicia Wildfire knew all this. Ever since Bearon Weimar had returned from Bearkingdom-Palace he hadn't stopped crowing about the success of their plot to overthrow King Antonius and Queen Dearie. By now, she knew, the former king and queen would be in exile on a bleak and forlorn place called Wight-Island.

'Means-which Chancellor-new needed-is,' said Bearon Weimar's visitor.

Alicia saw the bearon's eyes flicker. His guest had raised an important subject. Bearon Weimar had been prowling back and forth muttering to himself about it constantly. He'd concluded that of the four bearons, Herault and Sudbury could be ruled out as being too junior. That meant only himself and Bearon Drachenloch were in the running. Bearon Weimar's visitor had clearly worked this out too.

'Must-you favourite-be,' he said. 'With-together Bearon Drachenloch.'

'That true-is,' said Bearon Weimar.

His visitor wasted no time in coming straight to the point. 'Can-me you-help Drachenloch-beat.'

Bearon Weimar was a shrewd bear. Inside his heart may have been pounding with excitement, but outside he appeared as severe as ever. 'How?' he asked. 'And important-more...why?'

'Why?' snapped the other bear angrily. 'That simple-is. Work-me-once for Bearon Drachenloch. Until sack-him-me.'

'For-what?' asked Bearon Weimar.

'An accident-unfortunate,' replied his visitor. 'Lose-me saps-some.'

'Done-easily,' shrugged Bearon Weimar. Hadn't he lost his very own bruiser-big of a fighting-sap during the battle at Bearkingdom-Palace? 'From-where lose-you-them?'

The bear growled a long name that Bearon Weimar didn't completely catch – although Alicia Wildfire did. Even though she'd been expecting to hear it, the name still made her blood run cold. What the bearon did catch, though, was what his visitor said about the place he'd mentioned, 'Bearon Drachenloch it-run to money-make secret-top.'

Bearon Weimar's eyes widened, then glittered in anticipation. This was news-fantastic. Discovering a skeleton in Bearon Drachenloch's goblet-cabinet would be wonderful ammunition in his bid to become Chancellor.

'Money-make secret-top?' he echoed. 'Drachenloch told-not bear-any? It-kept self-to? Gave-not inclaw-tax to Chancellor Bruno?'

'Yes. No. Yes. No.' answered the other bear to these questions.

'Then think-me be-you-could helpful-*extremely*,'

smiled Bearon Weimar. 'Say-you again what called-was place-this? Slowly,' he added.

On her pedestal, Alicia Wildfire bit her lip and closed her eyes. She'd almost cried out the first time Bearon Weimar's visitor had said the name, and hearing it repeated was going to be even more painful.

'Name-official,' the huge bear growled, 'was Outpost-For Sap-Training, Education, Deployment. Name-common was Howling-Tower.'

'And name-you?'

Bearon Weimar's visitor threw his chest out proudly, just as he had when his word had been law in the Howling-Tower.

'Dictatum!' he barked. *'Inspector* Dictatum!'

Hidden outside, and not knowing who was inside with Bearon Weimar or how long they'd be, all Duncan Wildfire could do was to plan ahead.

'I need to get inside that den, Roger,' he said.

'But how do you know Bearon Weimar hasn't got lots of helper-bears?' said Roger Broadback. 'That's a big den.'

Duncan saw the sense in this. There was another problem, too. From what Benjamin had said, never-moves were always locked to their pedestals in some way. The same must be true of his Alicia or else she would have escaped long before now. Getting in to Bearon Weimar's den, therefore, was only half of the problem. He would have to come up with a quick way of releasing Alicia as well – or of giving himself enough time to do so slowly…

'A diversion, Roger! That's what I need.'

Roger smiled and nodded. He'd realised at once what Duncan was thinking. 'Such as…making so much noise that everybody inside rushes outside to see what's going on?'

'Giving me time to get inside while no one's looking,' nodded Duncan. 'And stay there for as long as it takes to find and free Alicia.'

'It will be a pleasure, my friend,' said Roger. 'Then I will use the trees we marked to follow our route back through the wood. When you have freed Alicia you can follow them too and we will meet up again.'

Duncan Wildfire clasped Roger Broadback's hand in gratitude. 'Thank you, Roger.'

Roger smiled again, but his smile was soon replaced by a look of concern. He pointed across at the forbidding entrance to Bearon Weimar's huge den.

'But – *how* will you get in, Duncan? Even if I produce the noisiest diversion imaginable, it will be almost impossible to run in that way without being seen.'

'Which is why I don't intend to get in that way,' laughed Roger. 'Don't you remember how we first knew who owned this den? What we saw?'

'The portrait on the roof?' said Roger, unsure what Duncan Wildfire was driving at.

Duncan was nodding. 'The portrait with the *glass eye*,

Roger. That eye can only be a window – and windows can be prised open or broken. When your diversion starts, I will be on that roof!'

Now Roger's smile returned. 'Then when do I begin, my friend? Now?'

'Not just yet. I don't want that door opening while I'm climbing up to the roof,' said Duncan. 'Let's wait until Bearon Weimar's visitor leaves.'

And so they settled down in their hiding place to wait for that to happen.

Bearon Weimar's visitor was finding that things weren't going quite as smoothly as he'd hoped. Inspector Dictatum was being asked to recount more of what had been going on at the Howling-Tower than he'd wanted.

'And…precisely-how money-made?' asked Bearon Weimar.

'Lotion-formulas, potion-formulas,' mumbled Inspector Dictatum almost inaudibly. The last thing he wanted was to be quizzed about the terrible methods he used in testing those formulas. His voice only rose to a normal level as he added, 'And sap-sales.'

'Sap-sales?' Bearon Weimar looked intrigued.

'Only times-some,' blustered Inspector Dictatum. 'Often-not.'

Bearon Weimar rubbed his chin thoughtfully. 'Often need-me saps,' he said. 'Where-you-sell?'

'Fleeceham-Market.'

On her pedestal, Alicia Wildfire felt weak and ill on hearing this reminder of where she'd been bought by King Antonius and Queen Dearie.

As for Inspector Dictatum, he was anxious not to get into any further details of the disastrous end to his time at the Howling-Tower. Unfortunately, in trying to change the subject, he now asked precisely the wrong thing.

'Been-you to Fleeceham-Market, Bearon Weimar?'

'Mind-you business-own!' snapped the bearon.

Shocked, Inspector Dictatum spread his huge arms wide. His viciously-sharp claws glinted. 'Sorry-me. Meant-me offence-none.'

But Bearon Weimar had taken more than offence. The question had raised a nasty suspicion about why Inspector Dictatum should ask if he'd ever sap-bought at Fleeceham-Market – a place which was, as they both well knew, in Bearon Drachenloch's region of Bear Kingdom.

'How know-me not-you a sneak-spy?' snapped the bearon suddenly. 'A sneak-spy here-sent cover-under by Drachenloch to out-find me-about?'

Having taken root, this thought grew rapidly in Bearon Weimar's mind. If he was looking for a way to cause trouble for Bearon Drachenloch, then wouldn't Bearon Drachenloch be looking for a way of doing exactly the same to him? He would. And what better way than sending one of his boss-bears on a sneak-spying mission!

His white muzzle twitching with mounting distrust, Bearon Weimar pointed his four-clawed paw at

Inspector Dictatum, and repeated his question. 'Eh? How know-me not-you a sneak-spy?'

Inspector Dictatum was lost for words. His was a feeble brain, and in concocting his plan to get revenge on Bearon Drachenloch for dismissing him after he'd found out about the saps who'd escaped from the Howling-Tower, he hadn't considered for a moment the possibility that Bearon Weimar wouldn't believe him. And as for *proving* he wasn't a sneak-spy – well, that was completely beyond him.

As for the suspicious Bearon Weimar, he took Inspector Dictatum's silence as clear proof that he was guilty as charged. If this great lumbering bear wasn't a sneak-spy then he'd have said so, wouldn't he?

'Out-get!' he snapped. 'Tell-you Bearon Drachenloch not-she me-fool!'

'But—' began Inspector Dictatum, finally finding his tongue.

'Buts-none!' shouted Bearon Weimar. 'Have-me evidence. There!'

With that he pointed a long claw straight at Alicia, his favourite red-haired never-move, standing motionless on her pedestal in the corner. As Inspector Dictatum's huge head swung round and his evil black eyes fixed themselves on her, Alicia's heart pounded so fearfully it felt as if it was about to burst. If the great bear recognised her...

But Inspector Dictatum showed no sign of having

done so. He seemed to be having trouble following Bearon Weimar's argument.

'Won-her-me from King Antonius,' the bearon was saying. 'And King Antonius her-bought from Fleeceham-Market. If Bearon Drachenloch her-sell, the king know-would!'

This was a completely ridiculous argument, of course. There was no rule saying that the buyer of a sap had the right to know the name of their previous owner. But Inspector Dictatum was too slow and stupid to think of this. The only thought plodding through his mind was that his plan was in ruins. And if Bearon Weimar questioned him even further then the whole truth might come out: that Bearon Drachenloch had known absolutely nothing about the evil things the Inspector had been doing at the Howling-Tower.

Inspector Dictatum rose to his feet, his ears almost touching the glass window set into the ceiling of the entertaining-chamber. 'Making-you mistake-big,' he growled defiantly.

'Think-me-not!' snapped Bearon Weimar. 'Now out-get!'

Scowling, Inspector Dictatum turned on his heel. He took one last, lingering look at the never-move on her pedestal in the corner, frowned for a few moments, then stomped out of Bearon Weimar's den and away.

Duncan Wildfire took some time to recover from the shock of seeing who Bearon Weimar's visitor had been.

Never in his whole life had he wanted to see that evil bear again. His only consolation was that – judging by the furious look on Inspector Dictatum's face and the speed with which he'd hurried away – it didn't appear likely that he'd be coming back soon.

In the event, this delay worked in his favour. Had he started immediately on his plan to climb up onto the roof of Bearon Weimar's den he would undoubtedly have been caught. For, not long after Inspector Dictatum's angry departure, the front door opened and Bearon Weimar himself padded out. An excited young bear was scurrying beside him: his daughter-cub, Filia.

'Can-me trees-climb, Papa?' she squealed.

'Course-of, heart-sweet!' smiled Bearon Weimar. 'If care-you-take.' And lifting his daughter-cub into his arms, he rubbed his snout playfully on hers.

It is a curious fact that the most awful parents can produce the most delightful cubs (the same goes for delightful parents and awful cubs, of course) and in Bearon Weimar's case this is was exactly so. Filia Weimar was as honest and cheerful as her father was scheming and grim. She was also as playful and untidy as her mother was prim and proper.

Lady Weimar was the next to emerge from the den. A pampered she-bear with rings on every claw, she immediately began to look this way and that while tapping one paw impatiently on the ground. This she did until, rattling up from somewhere behind the den, two large carts appeared. Both were covered with canopies of thatched straw and pulled by teams of blank-eyed humans.

Bearon and Lady Weimar climbed aboard the first cart. Various helper-bears appeared, carrying hampers which they loaded into the second cart before climbing aboard themselves.

'Return-we in sun-comes-two,' barked Bearon Weimar to a lone helper-bear (called Forthold) standing at the den door. And then, with a crack of his rope whip, the poor cart-saps heaved and pulled and rattled them all slowly away.

Duncan Wildfire watched them go with mixed feelings. How he would have loved to set those poor cart-saps free! It wasn't possible, of course. But rescuing his beloved Alicia suddenly seemed to have become *very* possible. It looked as if most of the den's occupants had gone off in the carts. Not only that, from what Bearon Weimar had said, they were going to be gone for a whole two sun-comes. Duncan's spirit soared at the thought.

Hard as it was, he waited for some time after the travel-carts trundled away, just in case they should return unexpectedly. When they didn't, Duncan knew that there would never be a better time to launch his rescue bid.

'Do I still need to create a diversion?' whispered Roger. 'There might only be one bear left in the place now.'

'I don't know yet,' said Duncan. 'I'll get up on the roof first. I might be able to see more through that window.'

And so, leaving Roger where he was, Duncan crept stealthily out from their hiding place…

THE RESCUE

Duncan and Roger hadn't been the only ones relieved to see Bearon Weimar and the others go off on their trip. Still shackled to her pedestal in the entertaining-chamber, Alicia had been glad to see the bearon go as well. She knew that it meant she would soon be released. Not only was her owner a suspicious and ambitious bear, he was also selfish and vain. His selfish view was that his never-moves had to stay in position only while he was around because, his vanity told him, that he and he alone was cultured enough to fully appreciate their beauty.

Sure enough, not that long after the Weimar travel-cart had rattled away, Forthold the helper-bear padded in to release Alicia from her shackles. What he should do now, he knew, was take her back to the secure alcove at the far side of the den where Alicia and the other never-moves were kept while not on duty. But he'd been left on his own and whenever that rarity occurred, Forthold's number one priority was to get his head down for a quiet snooze.

'Up-you-lock later,' he muttered to Alicia. 'Here safe-you-be. That door-front too-far heavy-much for sap-woman.' Then away he padded.

Alone, Alicia sat on her pedestal and rubbed life back into her aching limbs. She dried her tears – the tears she'd shed every day since being bought at Fleeceham-Market and forced into the life of a never-move. She didn't even consider trying to open the heavy front door which opened directly into the entertaining-chamber. Forthold was right. Opening that door on her own would be completely impossible. Alicia settled instead for the sheer delight of being able to walk around freely…

Outside, Duncan was hurrying across to Bearon Weimar's den; but *not* towards the front entrance. His target was at the side.

The bearon had spent quite a lot of money on having his den specially designed to look not as new, but as *old* as possible. A den which looked like the sort of cave one's fore-bears had lived in, *that* was the height of fashion for a bear of importance. In Bearon Weimar's case, this effect had been achieved by surrounding most of his den with jumbled piles of old rocks and boulders. It was one of these piles, reaching much of the way up towards the roof, that Duncan Wildfire had seen.

Quickly and quietly he began climbing from boulder to boulder and rock to rock. In next to no time he'd reached the top of the pile. He reached up, feeling with his fingers until he'd got a firm grip on the surface of the roof. And then, with a quick spring, he was clambering the rest of the way.

Down below, Duncan saw Roger Broadback pop his head out of his hiding place to give him a broad grin and thrust a thumb in the air. Duncan now looked across the surface of the roof. This close up, Bearon Weimar's portrait didn't look like a portrait at all. It simply looked as though the wooden roof was covered in gouges and claw-gashes, each of which had been stained either black or silvery-grey. There was only one thing that bore some resemblance to what they'd seen from the top of the hill: the window that formed the portrait's single eye. For there it was, glinting on a section of roof almost directly above the front door. Without hesitation, Duncan crouch-crawled across the roof until he'd almost reached it. Then, laying flat on his stomach, he slithered the last short part of the way – and looked down...

Inspector Dictatum was sulking. After being sent on his way by Bearon Weimar, he stormed straight out to the cart-way and begun to climb the hill. He had little choice now but to go back to the region of End-East, to Bearon Drachenloch. Perhaps he could think of a way of getting back into his favour?

But Inspector Dictatum had found all the thinking

he'd been doing very exhausting indeed. By the time he'd reached the top of the hill his head was sore. Seeing the by-lay at the side of the cart-way he'd decided what he needed now was a lie down and a good sulk.

So he lay and sulked and sulked and lay until he finally decided it was time to leave Bearon Weimar's territory for ever. But, before he went, he couldn't help but take a last bitter look at that suspicious bear's face.

Getting to his feet, he gazed down the hill at the roof of Bearon Weimar's den and cursed the bearon's portrait. He cursed its silver-grey fur. He cursed its white muzzle. He cursed its twinkling window of an eye...

Its *smudged* window of an eye?

For, as he'd looked and cursed, that twinkling eye had suddenly become partly covered by an oddly-shaped blotch. Inspector Dictatum's evil yellow eyes narrowed into a squint. Slowly the oddly-shaped blotch became sharper – and he saw that it was...a sap-shape! A sap must have climbed onto the roof of Bearon Weimar's den and was now looking down through its window!

But – at what? What in that den could possibly be of interest to a sap? The answer came to him in the sort of flash that Inspector Dictatum had rarely experienced. The one thing of interest to a sap could only be Bearon Weimar's never-move, who...he'd seen before! He'd thought she looked familiar. Of course! It was the Wildfire woman, Alicia, the one whose husband had been the first to escape from the Howling-Tower, before his accursed hair-red son had turned up.

And the husband! Duncan Wildfire! He'd tried to rescue his wife before. Could it be that he was trying to do it again?

Inspector Dictatum sulked for not a moment longer. Instead he began to thunder down the hill as fast as his four sharp-clawed paws would carry him.

In Bearon Weimar's entertaining-chamber, Alicia had stopped walking about. She was sitting on her pedestal, running her stone-painted fingers through her lustrous red hair and thinking again of her dear husband Duncan, and of Benjamin, her long-lost son. If she closed her eyes, she could almost see them.

'Alicia!'

Sometimes she could almost hear their voices, so real were they to her.

'Alicia! It's me, your Duncan!'

Alicia smiled ruefully. Her husband had never simply called himself just by his name. It was always 'your Duncan'. Oh, how she missed him!

And she might have gone on dreaming of her husband's voice had it not been joined by a fierce hammering on the little window in the ceiling. Startled, Alicia looked up – and saw her husband looking down!

'Duncan!' she cried. 'Oh, Duncan!'

On the roof, Duncan Wildfire was elated. Not only

had he found his dear wife, he could see that she wasn't tied or chained to anything. That could make rescuing her so much simpler.

'Alicia!' he shouted. 'Are there any bears guarding you?'

'Just one,' cried Alicia. 'And I'm sure he's asleep somewhere.'

'Is the entrance door locked?' shouted Duncan.

'No. But it's far too heavy for me to open on my own.'

'Then you pull, while Roger and I push!' shouted Duncan.

Back he went across the roof, as quickly as he was able. As he ran he beckoned to Roger Broadback to come out from his hiding place. By the time Duncan had clambered down the pile of boulders, jumped to the ground, then raced across to the entrance, Roger was there waiting for him.

Duncan hammered on the huge front door. 'Alicia! When I count to three, pull. At the same time, Roger and I will push with all our might!'

Roger Broadback nodded. Leaning his shoulder against the door, he braced his legs ready to push hard. Beside him, Duncan did the same. Then on his count of 'One, two – three!' Duncan and Roger pushed furiously against the door. It moved only slightly, but it was enough to cause Alicia to cry out from inside, 'It's opening! Try again!'

Gritting their teeth with the effort, Roger and

Duncan pushed with all their might. The door opened a little further, enough for them to be able to see a strip of pale entertaining-chamber wall.

'Let's take a run at it,' urged Roger Broadback.

This they did. Stepping back a few paces, Duncan and Roger raced forward and threw themselves against the solid wood. The door moved. Wild with hope, they found the strength to try again, and again – the gap at the side of the door grew large enough to allow Alicia's fingers to wrap round the edge. Now she could help by pulling at the weighty door with all her might.

Her efforts made that extra bit of difference. As the door swung further open, the gap became large enough for Duncan to squeeze through and immediately take his dear wife into his arms. Roger Broadback simply stood and watched, a huge smile on his face.

Then, without any warning, he found himself being thrust into Bearon Weimar's entertaining-chamber to join them. Alerted by Roger's cry of surprise, Duncan and Alicia swung round. But by then the heavy door had already been slammed shut again.

'What's happening, Duncan?' cried Alicia.

The answer came immediately. From the other side of the door, came a sound they'd hoped never to hear again – a sound which began as a chuff-puff, built to a hiss-growl and finally turned into a shattering roar.

The sound made by the most terrifying bear they'd ever known.

Inspector Dictatum.

A *triumphant* Inspector Dictatum.

THE FLOPPING-BOARD

Benjamin, Mops and Spike were ready to begin exploring Hide-Park. After a good meal they'd asked Only Armstrong (who was so tickled by Mops's new first name for him that he'd started using it himself) to tell them all he could about the layout of Hide-Park.

Only shrugged. 'Haven't really looked,' he said. 'None of us have. We eat, we sit or we play near the cabins, then we go through the trees to the big field to chase around, then we come back and have a rest till we're hungry. Then we do it all over again.'

'Dear me, Only,' said Mops, 'nobody could accuse you of being wildly adventurous, could they?'

Only Armstrong shrugged. 'Why go looking for trouble?' he said.

'Trouble?' said Benjamin. 'Why do you say that?'

'Mrs Dumpling says she's heard there *are* bears in Hide-Park. Nasty ones. Go where you shouldn't and they tear you to bits.'

'How does she know?' asked Spike.

'Mary Graceful told her.'

'And how does *she* know if none of you have ever been out exploring?' asked Mops.

Only frowned. 'Er...I don't know.'

And so, very little the wiser, Benjamin, Mops and Spike set off. As the one useful thing they'd learned was that the rough pathway leading away from the glade took them to the chasing-field, they decided to follow that.

It brought them out to the huge open space on which they'd seen children running and playing when they'd first looked down on Hide-Park – the same space that Only Armstrong had said they called 'the chasing-field'. Now they saw again that this chasing-field ran the whole width of Hide-Park, from the steep rock wall on one side to the chasm on the other; also far ahead, to where it reached around both sides of the gold-leafed forest.

For a while Benjamin, Mops and Spike simply ran, skipped, jumped and turned somersaults for the sheer delight of being free. They then decided to walk all the way over to the rock wall to see whether it really was as impossible to climb as it had looked from outside. It was. The rock was slippery and the wall so high that it made them feel even tinier than when they were forced to get close to a bear.

But their days of getting close to bears were over! As this wonderful thought returned, they ran all the way back to where the other children, together with a few grown-olders like Belinda Dumpling, had come out of the chasing-field. There they lazed and relaxed until just after middle-sun, when everybody began to drift back towards the glade for food and drink.

It was wonderful – so wonderful that, when everybody else decided to stay in the glade after their meal, Benjamin, Mops and Spike returned to the chasing-field. This time they began to walk in the opposite direction, towards the hummock-dotted side of the valley. From the other side of the chasing-field the hummocks had been so far away that they'd almost melted into the surrounding grassland. Now much nearer, they were surprised to discover just how evenly they were spaced. So, too, were they surprised to discover that the ground beneath their feet changed from being flat and level to sloping sharply downwards.

Mops suddenly let loose a cry of happiness. 'I'm going to roll!'

Throwing herself onto the warm grass she began to do just that. Shaking their heads and laughing, Benjamin and Spike watched her go.

'Mad,' grinned Benjamin. 'She'll be so dizzy she won't be able to stand up when she reaches the bottom—'

He choked on his words as a sudden, awful realisation struck him. They were now so close to the hummock-lined side of the valley that there could be one only thing at the bottom of the slope…

'The chasm!' he screamed, as he began to run after Mops.

With Spike close behind, Benjamin sprinted as fast as he could. Ahead of him, Mops was still squealing and rolling. But beyond her, the bottom of the slope was now close enough for them to see the yawning gap between where it ended and the side of the valley began to rise again.

'Stop!' screamed Benjamin. 'You'll go into the chasm!'

He was getting closer, but not close enough for Mops to hear. With a massive effort, Benjamin tried to go even faster. But going faster while running downhill was too much. Suddenly it seemed as if his legs couldn't keep up with the rest of his body. He stumbled badly – then toppled over completely, his arms and legs flying into the air as he landed on the ground. Moments later, Spike was crashing into him and landing in a heap.

Stunned and dizzy, Benjamin looked up. Ahead, Mops was still rolling and squealing. But suddenly she disappeared from sight. Her squeal turned into the briefest of screams.

Then everything went quiet.

Dazed and fearful, Benjamin and Spike crawled forward on their hands and knees. The other side of the chasm came into view, followed by more and more of its sheer rock side until finally they could go no further. Dry-mouthed, and dreading what they were about to see, they peered over the edge…

'Well,' said a sharp voice, 'I don't think I'll do *that* again!'

'Mops!' cried Benjamin with relief. 'You're safe!'

Mops had been extraordinarily lucky. Both to their left and to their right, the chasm plummeted straight down. But *not* at the point where she had toppled over. There, just below the edge, a kind of platform jutted out from the sheer side. Mops had landed on it and – although badly winded and very, very dizzy – had fallen no further.

'Are you two going to help me up, then?' she said finally, standing on tip-toes and reaching up towards them.

Benjamin and Spike leaned down, each taking one of Mops's hands, and hauled her up to safety. She sat down beside them and gave a sigh of relief. The whole experience had clearly terrified her more than she was letting on, for she showed no sign of moving for some time.

While he waited, Benjamin studied the platform Mops had luckily landed on. It was made of a single, claw-sliced piece of acorn-wood about two paces in length. Its near end had been firmly jammed into a wide crack in the rock of the chasm's side. But what was it for? It wasn't wide enough to be a bridge, nor did it reach anywhere near to the far side of the chasm. The platform looked old and weatherbeaten, but its far end wasn't jagged – so it had never had been a bridge that had snapped some time in the past. So what was it for? Intrigued, he asked Spike if he had any ideas.

'Simple, matey. It's called a flopping-board.'

'A *what*?'

'Remember what I told you when we first met in that Howling-Tower? That my owners slung me in the river when they didn't want me any more?' He pointed at the platform. 'Well to make sure I went right into a deep bit, they forced me to the end of one of those. That's what they're used for. Bears love flopping off them into the water.'

'Excuse me for pointing out an *itsy-bitsy* flaw in that perfectly splendid explanation,' said Mops, showing signs of recovery from her ordeal. 'But any bear flopping off that particular board would end up dead at the bottom of the chasm.'

'They would *now*,' said Spike.

'And what's that supposed to mean?' asked Mops.

Benjamin knew. 'The only thing it can mean, right Spike? That the chasm wasn't always like this. That it used to be filled with water.'

THE TULIP-TREE

After her narrow escape at the chasm, Mops had wanted nothing more than to return to their cosy cabin and get a good night's sleep. Benjamin and Spike were happy to agree. After all, they had all the time in Bear Kingdom to go out and explore their new home.

And so they'd gone back and spent a pleasant sun-go chatting to Only Armstrong and the others. They'd found out some interesting things. Penelope Curls and Oliver Spindle, the two children they'd seen arrive in a sack, weren't the only ones to have encountered Bearon Weimar.

'He bought me, too,' said tall, long-legged Mary Graceful. 'I thought he wanted me as a never-move but instead he sent me here. I heard him say to my owner: "will-she us-give a run-good for money-our!" – whatever that meant.'

Hearing this, Belinda Dumpling, the podgy grown-older, gave a gasp of surprise. 'Well, I never did! He told my owner almost the same thing. Except that he said I'd give them a run-easy.' She scooped up another handful of nuts and berries and pushed them into her mouth. 'I didn't have a clue what he was talking about either,' she mumbled.

Very few of the humans had found Hide-Park for themselves. Instead, one after another, most of them said something similar to Mary Graceful and Belinda Dumpling. They'd been bought by Bearon Weimar, who'd then had them taken to Hide-Park. Only one had a different story to tell, a wheezing grown-older named Albert Gaptooth who said he'd been in Hide-Park for three moons.

'Bearon Weimar didn't buy me,' he added slowly. 'He didn't have to. He already owned me.'

'Really?' asked Benjamin, quickly. 'What did you do?'

'I was a cart-sap!' interrupted Albert Gaptooth. 'I helped pull his carts, sun-come after sun-come, until I was too old and weary to do it any more.'

Spike looked at him and smiled ruefully. 'You might have been pulling the cart I hid on when I got caught and turned into Bearon Weimar's fighting-sap.'

Unsurprisingly, there was one question Benjamin was desperate to ask. 'Did you once see a never-move arrive? A beautiful lady with red hair...'

'I really don't want to talk about it!' snapped Albert Gaptooth. He struggled irritably to his feet. 'I don't even want to think about it. These past three moons have helped me begin to forget I ever was a cart-sap. Sending me here was the first kindness

Bearon Weimar ever showed me. I've got to be grateful to him for that. So no more questions!'

Benjamin, Mops and Spike awoke to the sound of the wind moaning through the trees and buffeting the windows of their cabins. Outside, swirls of golden leaves were chasing each other in circles.

'Oh, I just *love* walking in the wind!' trilled Mops. 'Let's go exploring again today.'

'But nowhere near the chasm, eh Squawker?' grinned Spike.

They set off after their meal. But when they reached the open spaces of the chasing-field this time they didn't stop to run free. Neither did they turn left or right and walk towards the sides of Hide-Park. Instead they headed straight on, towards the forest in the far distance.

Every now and then, Mops would close her eyes, turn her face to the wind and shout, 'We're free!' at the top of her voice. At this, a surge of joy would sweep through Benjamin and he'd laugh delightedly. His dreams had come true – they were free!

They'd been walking for some while before Spike made his own small contribution. When Mops cried, 'We're free!' yet again, he thrust his hand out and said, 'And soon we'll be getting wet.'

The strengthening wind had brought some thick dark clouds with it. The first few fat blobs of rain had begun to fall. It was only then, as Benjamin thought about taking shelter, that he realised just how far they'd walked. The trees surrounding the glade were very far away, the other children just moving dots as they hurried back to the dry cabins. He, Mops and Spike were much closer to the edge of the forest.

'How about taking cover in there?' he suggested, though without enthusiasm.

Close up the huge forest, so attractive and golden from far away, looked quite different. The close-packed trees made it appear much darker and really quite forbidding. The dark grey skies glowering above the treetops only added to the unwelcoming feel of it.

Spike clearly wasn't keen. 'Gah! Who's bothered about a little rain?' he snorted, trying to make a joke of it.

'I am!' retorted Mops. 'I have only just got my hair back into some kind of style!'

All too soon the rain was coming come down in wind-blown sheets. They knew then that they had little choice. Running hard, their hands over their heads, Benjamin, Spike and an irritably bedraggled Mops scampered reluctantly to the shelter of the forest.

They ventured in – not far, but far enough to be out of the reach of the gusting rain. They found themselves surrounded by a gloomy darkness. The trees were tall and ancient. So closely were they growing together that hardly any of the grey sky could be seen above their tops.

Benjamin shivered. If Belinda Dumpling's silly rumour about places to avoid was in any way true, then this forest — even from the little he'd seen of it — was likely to be top of the list.

'Stick together,' he said.

'That goes without saying,' shuddered Mops, 'though I'm glad you said it.'

'Agreed,' said Spike.

They then heard three different sounds, one after the other. First, a distant rumble of thunder. This was quickly followed by the whine of the wind, gusting between and above the swaying trees. Then, thirdly, a high-pitched cry of fear.

'One of the others must be in here!' said Mops, wide-eyed.

Spike shook his head. 'Who? We left them all behind. And they all said they don't explore, didn't they?'

Benjamin knew what Spike was getting at. But there'd been something different about the cry they'd heard. 'But that didn't sound like a bear, Spike,' he said. 'It sounded like a human.'

He edged further into the forest, following a wide, leaf-covered track in the direction of the cry. Spike and Mops followed warily behind, glancing this way and that as they moved.

And then, as the wind gusted again, they heard the cry once more: high-pitched, mingling in with the moaning wind and creaking branches, but a cry which came down to them quite clearly.

Yes, *down* to them. For, without a shadow of a doubt, the cry had come from high above their heads.

'Somebody's stuck up a tree,' said Benjamin. 'We've got to help them.'

'Well we can't do that until we *find* them!' said Mops. Raising her cupped hands to her mouth she tilted her head back and called out. 'Where are you?'

Mixed with the sound of the wind and another rumble of thunder, the high-pitched wail she got back wasn't in the slightest bit intelligible. But it did at least tell them one thing: roughly where to look.

The sound seemed to have come from not too far ahead. Led by Benjamin, they ran on and found themselves in a small clearing. There, alone in the centre, stood a tree shaped like a tulip-flower. It had been cut off at its base many, many summers before, and four shoots had sprouted in the place of the single trunk. These four shoots, thick and gnarled, now soared so high up into a swaying canopy of yellowing leaves that their tops were out of sight.

Mops called again. 'Where are you?'

She was answered by a wail of sheer terror, for at that moment a crack of lightning split the air. Benjamin looked up. As the branches of the tulip-tree swayed alarmingly he caught the faintest glimpse of black amongst the greens, yellows and browns.

'He's up there!' shouted Benjamin, sprinting over

to the thickest of the tree's four trunks.

Mops went after him and clutched at his arm. 'What are you *doing*?'

Benjamin shook himself free. 'I'm going to climb up and help him. He could fall.'

'Yes, on *you*!' cried Mops. 'Come back, Benjamin!'

But, using one of the other trunks of the tulip-tree as support, Benjamin was already climbing steadily upwards.

'Be careful, matey,' called Spike.

Up Benjamin went, feeling the tulip-tree begin to sway as he rose higher and the wind grew stronger. Whoever was above him had obviously climbed higher than he meant to and was frozen with fear. The danger now was that the stronger the wind got, the more he'd try to cling on – until his strength finally ran out. Benjamin climbed as quickly as he could. Above him, the small branches which jutted out from each of the four trunks of the tulip-tree were being blown back and forth. Dying leaves showered down towards him. All Benjamin could do now was to head steadily towards the patch of black he glimpsed every so often.

He was perhaps two-thirds of the way up the swaying tree trunk when another crack of lightning split the air. It was followed, after the shortest of gaps, by a deep and rolling burst of thunder.

The cry of fear that now came from above Benjamin was almost a shriek. 'Me-help! Me-help!'

Me-help?

Benjamin looked up. As the branches above his head swayed back and forth the patch of black grew…and he saw for the first time who – or, rather, *what* – he was trying to save. A young, black bear-cub. A female, judging from her size, and just as well. The uppermost part of the trunk she was clinging to, her claws digging deep into the bark, would have snapped under the weight of a bigger, heavier male-cub.

But male or female – did it matter? What was he doing, trying to save a *bear-cub*?

Benjamin almost turned back. But the trunk was now bending with the cub's weight and the rising wind was making it worse. If it bent much more it would surely snap, sending the cub plummeting to earth – and him with it. Bnjamin had no choice. He could be in more danger if he didn't save her than if he did.

'Hold on!' he cried, hoping the cub would realise that he was trying to help.

Swiftly he climbed higher, almost losing his own footing as a sudden sharp gust made the trunk he was climbing tremble and sway. But the cub was now within reach. She'd climbed the same one of the tulip-tree's four trunks as he, but climbed up far too high, up to where the trunk was dangerously thinner. Benjamin beckoned furiously, hoping that she would realise that he was telling her to begin climbing down towards him.

'Too-frightened Filia-is!' came a terrified wail.

There was only one thing Benjamin could think of doing. He climbed higher still, until he was right beneath the trembling cub. She looked down at him with a pretty, white-muzzled face – but even this gentle movement caused the narrowed trunk to dip alarmingly. Desperately hanging on to it with one hand, Benjamin pointed to the ground far beneath them with the other.

'Follow me down!' he shouted above the moaning wind.

Filia looked doubtfully at Benjamin, unable to pluck up the courage to move. But another gust of wind, the fiercest yet, changed all that. As a nearby branch snapped off with a wicked crack, the cub saw that it was only a matter of time before the same thing would happen to the part of the tree she was clinging to. With a whimper and a shudder, Filia hesitantly began to follow Benjamin downwards.

Benjamin went as slowly as he dared. Whenever the wind gusted and the trunk swayed, he stopped and held on tightly. Then, when it was calmer, he continued downwards, checking as he went that the she-cub was still following him. He saw that she was more than following; she seemed to be carefully making sure that she planted her paws in exactly the same spots that Benjamin placed his feet.

'Benjamin Wildfire,' he heard Mops screech suddenly. 'Are you totally mad? Risking your neck to rescue a bear-cub?'

Benjamin felt a surge of relief. If Mops could see them then they must be nearly halfway to the ground. Climbing down was getting easier too – for, being thicker, the lower part of the tulip-tree's trunk wasn't swaying anything like as much as the top.

Above him, it seemed as if the bear-cub was also growing in confidence. If anything, she was moving even quicker than Benjamin, showing just how a bear could use her claws to get down from a tree far faster than a human. As Benjamin paused to adjust his hand-hold at a slightly tricky part, one of the she-cub's sharp-clawed rear paws landed on Benjamin's fingers and gave them a painful dig.

'Hey, watch where you're treading!' yelled Benjamin without thinking.

'Sorry!' cried Filia. 'It was an accident!'

Benjamin looked down. They now had hardly any distance to go at all. Beneath him he could see Mops and Spike staring up at them, silent and open-mouthed. It took just a few more quick steps before he was leaping down to land on the springy earth beside them.

'Phew!' he said. 'I'm glad that's over.'

Neither Mops nor Spike replied. They continued goggling – at him, then at Filia the bear-cub as she too leapt to the ground.

For a moment the cub looked as though she was going to scamper away immediately. Then she turned, stood shakily upright, and looked at Benjamin.

'Thank-me-you, Benjamin Wildfire,' she said.

Benjamin, still awash with relief that they were both still in one piece, merely smiled and nodded. Filia smiled back at him. Then, dropping down to all fours, she raced away deep into the heart of the forest.

Benjamin watched her go, then turned back to Mops and Spike. They were still standing stock still and unnaturally silent. 'What's the matter?' he asked – though even as he spoke, Benjamin thought he knew what the problem was.

'Tha-that bear...' began Mops.

'Yes,' said Benjamin grimly. 'Belinda Dumpling was right. There *are* bears in Hide-Park.

Spike shook his head wildly. 'Not j-just that,' stammered Spike. 'That bear sp-spoke...'

Benjamin frowned. 'Of course it spoke. Bears *do* speak – and we can understand them.'

'B-but...' Mops said, '*she* could understand *you*!'

'What?'

Spike forced the words out. 'When you shouted, "Watch where you're treading!" that bear answered—'

'"Sorry! It was an accident!!"' breathed Benjamin, recalling exactly what Filia the bear-cub had replied. Up in the tulip-tree the moment had passed so quickly he hadn't thought anything of it. But now he realised the full enormity of what it meant. To have answered as she had, Filia *must* have understood what he'd said. Not only that...

'She thanked me,' said Benjamin.

'"Thank-me-you,"' said Mops. 'That's bear-speak. That's not important.'

'But it *is*!' cried Benjamin.

Spike frowned. 'How come?'

'Because it shows she *knew* we would understand her!'

There was no other explanation.

However unbelievable it seemed, Filia the bear-cub knew that humans understood bear-talk.

And she could talk human.

A CHANGE OF HEART

Inspector Dictatum had thoroughly enjoyed the two sun-comes since catching Duncan Wildfire and his sap-friend trying to free Duncan's sap-wife, Alicia. Having slammed Bearon Weimar's den door on the three of them, he'd picked up a couple of large boulders as if they were peas and rolled them in front of the door to stop it being opened again. He'd then roared until Forthold, the bearon's helper-bear, had appeared bleary-eyed, having been rudely awoken from a snooze he'd been having beneath a cosy nut-bush. Together they'd then gone in through a rear door to which Forthold had a key, chained and manacled the three saps, and finally shut them in the secure never-move's chamber where Alicia was normally kept on her own. It would be cramped and uncomfortable with three in it, but what did Inspector Dictatum care? Just so long as they couldn't get out. And, with the only light in the chamber coming from a high window that was far too small for any of the saps to squeeze through, he was satisfied that they couldn't.

Even so, from then on Inspector Dictatum had happily devoted himself to the tasks of patrolling and roaring. It had been just like old times in the Howling-Tower. All he needed now was for his cleverness to be recognised by Bearon Weimar.

He waited eagerly for the travel-carts to return. Finally he heard them clattering up towards the den, their gasping cart-saps looking as if they couldn't run a step further. Bearon Weimar had driven them hard. The work he'd been supervising in Hide-Park had all been finished, but it had been hard-going. The storm hadn't helped either. In fact he'd been so busy that he'd only realised his daughter-cub Filia had gone missing when she'd returned all wet and bedraggled. Lady Weimar had been less than pleased, and had spent most of the journey back telling him as much. So it was with extreme irritation that Bearon Weimar leapt down from the travel-cart to find himself snout-to-snout with Inspector Dictatum.

'Ordered-me-you to out-get!' he snapped.

Inspector Dictatum stood his ground. 'Will-you mind-change that-about soon-pretty,' he barked rudely.

'Why-me-should?' glowered Bearon Weimar.

'Because while away-you-were, stop-me cunning-saps away-taking your hair-red never-move.'

'What!' exploded Bearon Weimar, before his old suspicions returned. His eyes narrowed. 'It-prove.'

Inspector Dictatum gave a laugh-growl of

triumph. 'Will-it pleasure-be,' he smirked.

Then, puffed with pride, he led Bearon Weimar round to the barred and bolted never-move's chamber. Cramped and hungry, Duncan, Alicia and Roger heard them coming. They tensed themselves, ready to run out should the chamber's door open wide enough for them to get through. But, after Forthold had been called to unlock it, that door opened no wider than was necessary to allow Bearon Weimar's white-furred snout and beady eyes to peer round. Then it slammed shut again.

Having seen what he'd just seen, Bearon Weimar's suspicions vanished. His stunned face showed that he now realised Inspector Dictatum had been telling the truth. Seeing this, Inspector Dictatum pressed home his advantage.

'Knew-me before-seen your hair-red never-move. Name-her-is Alicia – Alicia *Wildfire*!' He spat out that last name with venom.

Before Bearon Weimar could respond, a young voice beside him cried out, 'Papa!'

'Quiet-be, Filia!' snapped Bearon Weimar. His inquisitive daughter-cub, now fully recovered from her ordeal, had followed them round to the never-move chamber. 'On-go, Inspector.'

Inspector Dictatum, delighted at the polite voice in which Bearon Weimar had spoken, was only too pleased to go on. 'Alicia Wildfire,' he said, 'a husband-has.

Name-him Duncan Wildfire. Them-both me-with in the Howling-Tower. Duncan Wildfire escape-did,' he growled bitterly.

But that was as nothing compared to the bitterness with which he added, 'As-also-did son-their, *Benjamin Wildfire*.'

'Papa! Papa!' squealed Filia.

'Quiet-be, say-me!' Bearon Weimar bellowed. 'Cubs should seen-be and heard-not!'

Inspector Dictatum ignored the interruption. His big moment had arrived.

'After-me out-thrown...' he paused, giving Bearon Weimar an aggrieved look so as to leave him in no doubt about how unjustly he thought he'd been treated, '...was-me home-returning when saw-me from top-hill the Duncan-sap roof-climbing and window-peering.'

'And added-you two-plus-two,' nodded Bearon Weimar, appreciatively.

'Four-getting!' snapped Inspector Dictatum. 'So back-me-run way-all them-catching pawed-red!'

Bearon Weimar took a deep breath. Admitting that he was wrong didn't come easily. He couldn't think of the last time he'd done it, if ever. But he had to admit it now.

'Apologies-my,' he said. 'Wrong-me you-about.'

Inspector Dictatum felt a little surge of pleasure. 'So, not-you think-me a Bearon Drachenloch sneak-spy?' he said.

'No,' smiled Bearon Weimar. 'Think-me useful-you.' He held out his four-clawed paw for Inspector Dictatum to clutch in a sign of forgiveness. 'No feelings-hard?'

Inspector Dictatum certainly did have hard feelings, but even his slow brain knew that it would be madness to say so. He shook his head. 'One-only feeling-hard have-me. The Duncan-sap accompanied-not by son-his, Benjamin Wildfire. Would-me-give paw-right to him-find.'

'Papa! Papa!' came the screech of a young bear just about bursting to have her say. This time Bearon Weimar relented.

'Yes, Filia daughter-my,' he sighed.

'Seen-me a Benjamin Wildfire! In Hide-Park!'

Inspector Dictatum reacted as if he'd been hit by lightning. His spine stiffened, his head swivelled on his thick neck, his evil eyes bulged and his foul yellow teeth opened in a terrifying grimace. It was all he could do to stop himself sweeping Filia off her feet and shaking her until she revealed every little detail. But stop himself he did. Filia was not just any daughter-cub, she was a bearon's daughter-cub. So instead he bent down and gave her what he hoped was a winning smile.

'Sure-you-am, pet-pop? Him-describe.'

'Hair-red,' said Filia, thinking carefully about what else she could say without letting slip how silly she'd been climbing to the top of a tree only to find that she couldn't get down. 'And climber-good!'

'Climber-good?' echoed Inspector Dictatum. The nightmare vision of Benjamin's tree-climbing, and its part in the break-out from the Howling-Tower, flashed through his mind. 'Benjamin Wildfire was climber-fantastic!' Another thought came to him. Could this cub be mistaken?

'How-you-know name-his?'

'Squeak-them-plenty,' said Filia, happy to have got off the subject of trees.

'Not-saying understand-you sap-speak!' growl-snorted Bearon Weimar.

Filia carefully avoided answering the question. 'Thought-me-heard like-something name-that friends-him-squeak, Papa. Could-me wrong-be, course-of.'

As for Inspector Dictatum, the question of whether Filia could or could not understand sap-speak didn't cross his mind. His only concern was that she certainly *wasn't* wrong. 'Friends-describe… if-would-you, angel-little,' he cooed, more for Bearon Weimar's benefit than for Filia's.

Filia thought. She hadn't noticed that much, not really. 'Was-one a girl-sap. Her-called "Mops". Body-little, voice-big. And…was-other a boy-sap. Him-called "Spike"!' Filia giggled delightfully. 'Was-him opposite-complete: body-big, voice-little!'

Inspector Dictatum had heard enough. Filia had just described the two who were with Benjamin Wildfire on that terrible night in the Howling-Tower. 'Them-is sure-for!' he snapped.

Bearon Weimar scratched his chin thoughtfully. A quite beautiful idea was forming in his devious mind. He already owned one hair-red sap: his never-move, Alicia. And now, under lock and key, he had another hair-red – the male-sap, Duncan.

'So...' he murmured, 'catch-me Benjamin Wildfire and would have-me hair-red family-complete!'

Inspector Dictatum bit his sizeable tongue. He was as keen as Bearon Weimar about catching Benjamin Wildfire, but not to give him the pleasure of owning the complete family. He wanted to catch Benjamin Wildfire for the sheer pleasure of ripping him into tiny pieces. So he simply bowed and said, 'Idea-wonderful, Bearon.'

But Bearon Weimar hadn't finished. 'Then give-me-them to King Bruno. Him-me-make Chancellor sure-for!'

'Idea-better-even,' lied Inspector Dictatum.

Bearon Weimar snapped his claws. Forthold the servant-bear came running. Quickly, Bearon Weimar rattled off a list of instructions. Inspector Dictatum was joining him and would be staying in the den. They would be making another trip to Hide-Park in two sun-comes' time. The hair-red saps had to be guarded with his life, but also looked after: they were valuable.

Finally, Forthold received his instructions about what to do with Roger Broadback. 'Him-release. Valuable-him-not.'

Forthold bowed deeply. 'Mean-you him-let away-run, Bearon?'

Bearon Weimar glowered. 'No! Cart-sap him-make.'

SAP-WATCHERS

Benjamin had been puzzling about Filia the bear-cub ever since he'd helped bring her to safety from the top of the tulip-tree. He was still puzzling a couple of sun-comes later. Had she really understood everything he'd said – or had it just seemed like it? Perhaps she'd guessed. But…she'd spoken his name, and thanked him! So, what if she really could understand and speak human? Did it matter? Talking about it in their cabin, Benjamin didn't really think it did.

Spike, though, was concerned about something else. 'What was she doing there, in that forest?' he asked.

'She probably just wandered over the bridge,' said Mops. 'Cubs will be cubs.'

Benjamin wasn't so sure. 'She's more likely to have come *with* another bear, Mops?'

Mops snapped her fingers as the answer came to her. 'One of Bearon Weimar's food-bringers, of course!' said Mops. 'They're the only bears we've seen.'

This statement, true until that moment, was about to be turned upside down. From outside came the sounds of shouting and running. Suddenly, Only Armstrong burst into their cabin.

'Bears!' he shouted. 'Hundreds of them! Thousands!'

Benjamin, Mops and Spike scrambled off their beds and raced outside. Were they in danger? It seemed not. The lovely glade was as quiet and peaceful as always. But, from somewhere beyond the trees, was coming a low, growl-rumbling noise they'd never heard before.

Having raised the alarm – if an alarm was what it was meant to be – Only Armstrong had raced off along the path which led to the chasing-field. Others were now doing the same, some quickly and some hesitantly. Benjamin suggested that it was better to follow than to stay. If the bears meant them harm then they would at least be in a position to run.

So through the trees they went, their feet kicking up golden leaves. But, unlike on every previous occasion, when they reached the end of the path they found that nobody had ventured onto the grass at all. They were all still clustered in the shelter of the trees, looking out towards the hummock-dotted side of the valley some two hundred paces away. Bears by the hundred (or possibly even by the thousand, as Only Armstrong had suggested) had begun to gather there.

'Let's get a closer look,' suggested Benjamin.

With Mops and Spike close behind, he began to thread his way through the trees, always keeping the side of the valley in view but never venturing out from cover. He stopped only when they'd reached the point at which the belt of trees ended, no more than twenty paces away from where the chasm began its sharp curve round towards the tree-trunk bridge.

Beyond the chasm, every hummock was crowded with bears. Most seemed to be in family groups, with grown bears lolling against the hummocks and excited cubs perched on their tops.

'What are they here for?' asked Spike nervously. 'To get us?'

'They'd by heading for that bridge if they were,' said Mops.

From where they were, they could just see the bottom of the track they'd followed from the cart-way. Bears were still streaming down to it – but none of them were heading towards the bridge either. Every bear seemed intent on finding a hummock of their own…

'It's almost as if those hummocks were built on purpose,' said Benjamin. 'So that the bears can use them to get a good view while they're…'

'While they're what?' asked Spike.

What had occurred to Benjamin didn't make a lot of sense, but it was the only explanation he could come up with. 'While they're watching us.'

'Watching us?' said Mops.

'Yes, just like that bear-cub said at Fleeceham Market, remember?'

Mops and Spike nodded solemnly. Fleeceham

Market was a place they'd been taken to from the Howling-Tower, supposedly to be sold. It was while they were there that a she-cub had noticed Benjamin's hair and squealed that it was just like that of a sap she'd been watching at Hide-Park. From then on, Mops and Spike had begun to believe, as Benjamin always had, that Hide-Park really did exist.

'That must be what these bears are doing,' said Benjamin. 'Having an outing to come and watch us.'

Mops shook her head in exasperation. 'But…watch us do what?'

'Anything,' answered Spike.

'How did you work that one out, pray?' snorted Mops.

'It's obvious, ennit?' replied Spike. 'If they've come to watch us like you say, then it don't matter what we do.'

And that did seem to be the case. As time went by, and not a single bear showed any signs of approaching the bridge across the chasm, a few of the children grew confident enough to venture out into the chasing-field. When they did, the watching bears immediately began to point and growl-shout. The voices carried clearly the short distance to where Benjamin, Mops and Spike were crouching.

'One-that's a legs-skinny!' they heard a young cub shout as a particularly thin girl ran out into view.

'And him a wobble-tum!' laughed another at the tubby boy who chased after her.

But that was about all. None of the watching bears got up or threw anything or ran towards the bridge. Like the careful bears who came in to fill the food hoppers it seemed as if they were trying their hardest not to be frightening. Benjamin glanced at Mops and shrugged. It seemed a peculiar way of spending their time, but if watching was all the bears wanted to do, then what was the point of them staying hidden?

'Shall we go out?' he asked.

Spike shook his head firmly. 'Not me, matey.'

'Why ever not?' said Mops.

'I don't like it,' muttered Spike. 'I don't like *them*. Bears sitting around watching us? It's not *natural*. They're not going to see me, ever.'

Mops sighed. 'You are so suspicious!'

'I don't care. There's too much going on round here I don't understand.'

'There's a lot you don't understand *anywhere*, not just around here!' snorted Mops. She fluffed up her hair. 'Well, I don't see a problem. If those bears have come especially to look at us humans, then I consider it my duty to make sure they don't go home without seeing the one and only me!'

And with that, out Mops went. What was more, she didn't simply turn and run up towards the wider part of the chasing-field. Instead she hopped and skipped straight over to where a large group of bears were sprawled around a hummock very close to the chasm.

As she drew near, some of the bears nudged each other. Mops stopped, giving them time to point her out to the rest of the group. Only then did she run forward, turn sideways without stopping, bend down, place her hands on the grassy ground, and execute one of the best cartwheels she'd ever managed. Her reward was a loud laugh-growl and much more pointing. A few bears even stood up to get a better view.

'I do believe they like me!' trilled Mops, looking back to where she'd left Benjamin and Spike.

Benjamin couldn't help laughing. Mops was showing off outrageously. After performing a few more cartwheels she'd then done a handstand against a tree. When that attracted another burst of laugh-growls, she ran around singing and dancing. It was as she ended her little show by doing the splits that Benjamin decided to go out and join her.

Spike laid a hand on his arm. 'Don't go, matey,' he said anxiously. 'Stay here.'

Benjamin shook his head. Most of the others had flooded outside now, running and playing themselves. The bears had come to watch them, no more than that. Spike's fears were ridiculous.

'I'm sure there's nothing to worry about, Spike,' said Benjamin. 'I'm going out.' And with that he left the shelter of the trees and raced across to join Mops.

'I think I'm their favourite!' she trilled as he ran up. The watching crowd's reaction to Benjamin's arrival, though, made her face fall. 'Well, I *was*.'

Almost as one, the bears had switched their attention from Mops to Benjamin. Excited shouts of young cubs carried to them across the chasm:

'Look-you at one-that!'

'A hair-red!'

'Before-never seen-me a hair-red!'

Mops smiled ruefully. 'Yes, they *definitely* like you the most. But then I can't say I blame them. I'd give my right arm for hair that colour.'

The babble of growl-shouting was growing. Young bears were standing on their parents' shoulders for a better view. But then a sudden commotion up at the top of the cart-track leading down into the valley made them look that way. To loud growl-bellows of 'Back-stand!' the stream of bears still flooding towards Hide-Park parted to let a travel-cart through.

The cart had clearly been driven hard, for the poor cart-saps harnessed to its front were on the point of exhaustion. With sodden hair plastered to their foreheads and looks of agony on their faces, even their own mothers wouldn't have recognised them. When the travel-cart finally halted on the wide, bare circle at the bottom of the track, every cart-sap slumped to the ground gasping for breath. They hardly stirred when, after releasing their chains, the cart-driver began to pass a bucket of water round for them to share.

'That's Bearon Weimar's helper-bear!' said Benjamin, seeing the distinctive patch of grey fur in the centre of the cart-driver's otherwise brown chest.

'Maybe he's brought more children here,' said Mops.

They saw very quickly that that was not the case. For, as the crowd was pushed back, a bear lumbered off the back of the travel-cart. Draped across his silvery-grey shoulders was a gold chain of office and, even from where they were, his white muzzle could be seen standing out in the centre of his face.

'Bearon Weimar!' gasped Benjamin.

He wanted to back away, towards the sanctuary of the trees. The last time Benjamin had seen him, Bearon Weimar had been in Bearkingdom-Palace, looking down at him and Spike in the evil fighting-pit. He was unlikely to have forgotten that they'd ruined the bearon's fun on that occasion. Neither would he have fond memories of Mops: he'd wanted her for a never-move and been rewarded for his trouble by a kick on the snout.

What stopped Benjamin running for cover was the discovery that Bearon Weimar hadn't been the only bear on board. A white-muzzled cub had leapt off and immediately been hoisted on to his broad shoulders.

'It's Filia, that cub you helped down from the tree!' cried Mops.

Benjamin's heart skipped a beat. What was she doing here? Could it be that he'd rescued Bearon Weimar's daughter-cub? A cub who, they suspected, could understand human talk? And now here they were, back again. Why?

That question was not to be answered. For even as Bearon Weimar began to carry Filia through to the very lip of the chasm, another bear emerged from the back of the travel-cart: a bear that Benjamin had seen only recently in his nightmares.

'Inspector Dictatum!' he cried in terror.

Beside him, Mops shrieked – and ran. Benjamin did the same then, turning and racing as fast as he could towards the shelter of the trees. For them to be caught again by Inspector Dictatum wouldn't just mean the end of their dreams of freedom – it would probably mean the end of their lives. And so, as they ran, not for a single moment did they look back.

Had they done so, they would have seen Filia point straight at the fleeing Benjamin.

They would have heard her cry loudly, 'There-is-he, Papa! Benjamin Wildfire!'

They would then have seen Bearon Weimar point with a four-clawed paw for the benefit of the bear who'd now lumbered to his side.

They would have seen that bear nod firmly.

And, finally, they would have seen the ugly smile of revenge which swept across the face of Inspector Dictatum.

THE TROPHY CHAMBER

Benjamin didn't know what to do for the best.

'If they're after us...' he began.

'You and Spike,' corrected Mops. 'It was you two who ruined Bearon Weimar's bet on the sap-fight at Bearkingdom-Palace.'

'Maybe Bearon Weimar's just after me,' said Spike, who'd been told the terrible news the moment that Benjamin and Mops crashed back into the trees beside him. 'I was his fighting-sap, remember.'

Another occurred to him. 'Or he could just be after you, Squawker. You were the one he wanted as a never-move.'

'It's all three of us, of course!' shouted Benjamin. 'Inspector Dictatum will see to that. I just can't work out what he's doing with Bearon Weimar.'

'Whatever it is,' said Spike, 'we can't stay here.'

Benjamin's heart sank. Spike was right. After all their struggles, after finding Hide-Park and discovering it was all that he'd dreamed it would be, it had become too dangerous for them to stay. But he simply couldn't leave Hide-Park, not yet.

'I've got to stay here, Spike. My father and mother are coming here to find me.'

Mops and Spike exchanged glances. It was Mops who put their thoughts into the most gentle words she could find. 'Benjamin, I... I don't think you should raise your hopes about that. It would have been hard enough for Duncan to rescue Alicia with just Bearon Weimar to cope with. But if he's had to deal with Inspector Dictatum as well...' She shook her head.

'I'm not leaving Hide-Park!' shouted Benjamin.

'But we can't *stay*!' insisted Mops. 'Tell him I'm right, Spike.'

'Well...' said Spike thoughtfully, 'you could *both* be right. Just because we can't stay, it don't mean we have to go.'

Mops clapped a hand to her head. 'Spike, I enjoy a good riddle as much as anybody – but now is not the time!'

'It's not a riddle,' insisted Spike. 'We can leave the glade, but still stay in Hide-Park. We just have to find somewhere else to hide for a while.'

'Ah! *Now* I understand,' said Mops, adding, to Spike's surprise, 'and I'm inclined to agree. Where do you suggest?'

It was Benjamin who answered. 'That forest.'

'What!' cried Mops. 'It could be crawling with bear-cubs like that Filia creature – not to mention their ferocious parents! That forest's the worst place we could go!'

Benjamin shook his head. 'That makes it the *best* place to go, Mops – because it'll be the last place they'll think of looking for us.'

Only Armstrong helped them load some food from the hoppers into a sack.

'You don't think they're after all of us, do you?' he asked.

Mops reassured him. 'No, just us. You'll all be safe. Safer, even, if we're not around. They won't pick on the rest of you if we've gone.'

They waited until sun-go was approaching, hoping that by then it would be too dark for them to be seen from beyond the chasm. Only Armstrong came with them as far as the chasing-field. Benjamin pointed out to him roughly where the tulip-tree was, telling him that was the direction in which they were heading. What he didn't say was that they had no idea what they would do when they reached it.

In the event, all they were capable of doing after the long, dark trek across the chasing-field was to bed down beside the four-trunked tree and try to get some sleep. Only when the first fingers of sun-come probed into the forest did they have a quick discussion about what to do next.

'Well, we can't stay here,' said Mops. 'Not in a spot

that ungrateful Filia cub knows. She could lead her father and Inspector Dictatum straight to us.'

'And it don't seem like a good idea to go that way,' said Spike, pointing the way Bearon Weimar's daughter had run after she'd thanked Benjamin.

Benjamin frowned. 'That doesn't leave us with much of a choice, does it?'

There were two other paths leading away from the area round the tulip-tree. One was well-worn and wide, like that which Filia had followed. The other was narrow and overgrown. Branches hung low overhead, brambles dangling menacingly from them. It looked as though it hadn't been used for ages – which, Benjamin decided, had to be a good thing.

Off they set. The path twisted and turned, but Benjamin was pretty certain that it was taking them up through Hide-Park, towards the big lake. Spike led. He'd armed himself with a piece of thick, broken branch which he used to hack aside any brambles which barred their way. For their part, Mops and Benjamin trampled hard on the creepers and grasses as they walked, flattening them so that they'd be able to make quicker progress if they came back this way again. At regular intervals, though, they'd pause and listen fearfully for any sound that suggested they were being followed.

Middle-sun came and went. By then, the three friends had built up something of a rhythm – so much so that they were almost on top of the large lodge before they saw it. It was standing on the edge of a beautiful, sheltered clearing. Its walls had been entirely made from acorn-tree logs, all chipped and shaped by builder-bear claws. Its sweeping, curved roof was made out of rushes and reeds. Across the whole width of its front was a wide, sun-facing verandah – perfect for lolling and snoozing.

What most attracted Benjamin's attention, though, was an object at the side of the porch. It looked as if it was the bottom part of a thick and solid tree-trunk, still rooted in the ground. Its top had been skilfully claw-carved into the shape of a bear's head – and not just any bear. The intricately worked chain of office round the bear's neck made clear exactly who it was meant to be.

'Bearon Weimar,' breathed Benjamin. 'But why's it here?'

'I suspect because – good or bad – that bear is impossibly vain,' said Mops. She turned to Spike. 'Didn't you say he had a portrait of himself on the roof of his den too?'

Spike nodded. 'Yeah. I saw it when he took me out for fights.' He shuddered at the painful memory. 'A big roof it was, an' all.'

'Big roof, big head,' sniffed Mops, giving the carved head an angry slap on its snout.

'You mean – this place is Bearon Weimar's?' said Spike, creeping up to the porch.

'No doubt about it. If his daughter-cub was here then it's almost certain that he was too. And as he's *far* too important to sleep in the open; he must have somewhere to bed down for the night whenever he visits, mustn't he? And this looks like the place.'

It looked as if Mops was right. Their path through the forest had brought them out at the side of the lodge. Creeping out further into the clearing, they now saw another, wider path leading all the way up to an arched opening at the front. What was more, it had obviously been recently used. Paw-prints littered the soft earth. Most were large, but some were small and cub-sized.

'I don't like it,' said Spike, backing away. 'They could all turn up here and find us.' Another, terrifying, thought struck him. 'They might even be inside!'

Mops shook her head. 'What, with all the noise you were making as you hacked through those brambles? They'd have surely been here waiting for us. Believe me, that place is empty.'

'Then we'd better look inside quickly, hadn't we?' said Benjamin grimly.

'What!' cried Mops. 'Why?'

'If this really is a den Bearon Weimar uses,' said Benjamin, 'then we might find something inside that's helpful.'

'In what way?' said Mops.

'I don't know!' shouted Benjamin.

'Come with me, Spike,' urged Benjamin.

'Excuse me, ladies first!' said Mops, pushing Spike to one side.

Spike frowned. 'Somebody should stay out here and keep watch.'

'Be my guest,' smiled Mops. 'But I have absolutely no intention of staying out here waiting for Inspector Dictatum to turn up and say hello. And if you've got any sense, neither should you.'

'Good point,' said Spike.

The arched opening was a kind of porch. A screen of rushes hung from the far end. Cautiously, their hearts in their mouths, Benjamin, Mops and Spike eased their way through it.

They found themselves in the lodge's main chamber. It was large and open. The smooth, bark-peeled walls were hung with torch-lights ready to be lit when dusk fell. Low acorn-wood tables were laden with roots and nuts and surrounded by comfy piles of straw all around. It looked like a chamber made for relaxing and talking, rather than sleeping. Various openings led off towards other chambers – bed-chambers perhaps, thought Benjamin. As he and Spike looked around the main chamber, Mops wandered through one of these openings.

It was her terrible, terrible scream that brought them running. They found her in a square, high-ceilinged chamber. She was trembling, one hand to her mouth while the other pointed shakily at what had been mounted on the walls.

Sap-wear. Laid out in neat rows, from floor to ceiling. There were shirts, shorts and socks. They were of varying sizes. Some were large, as if they'd been worn by a grown-older. Others were quite small, to fit a boy or girl younger than any of them. The items were all different colours, too. There were greens and blues and oranges and yellows. But, with all these differences, every piece of sap-wear on the walls had two things in common.

They were all blood-stained. And they all had groups of gaping slits with ragged edges.

The blood stains surrounded the slits which were sometimes in groups of three, sometimes in groups of four or five, as if the piece of clothing concerned had been cut apart by a set of sharp knives. But what Benjamin, Mops and Spike all knew, without saying, was that the cuts hadn't been caused by knives. They'd been caused by sets of bears' claws.

Beneath each shredded garment was a small wooden plaque. Words had been claw-engraved on them in fine, thin scratch-writing. Mops forced herself to bend and looked at one. It was beneath a boy's shirt – a shirt with five gaping shreds in the centre of its back.

'Wh...what does it say?' gulped Benjamin.

Mops took a deep breath. 'Male-sap,' she read slowly. 'Stones-seven, pebbles-three. By-hunted Bearon Drachenloch, fall-season in annum-second of King Antonius.'

Grimly, Spike pointed to another. This was beneath a girl's dress. Mops bent down to it.

'Female-sap,' she said quietly, tears trickling from the corners of her eyes, 'stones-five, pebbles-eleven. By-hunted Bearon Weimar, bud-season in annum-fourth of King Antonius.'

Benjamin gazed silently at the dress. It had four claw shreds in its back, with a gap where the fifth claw should have been.

Slowly Mops went round the chamber, reading every little plaque. They all carried the same information: whether the owner of the garment had been a boy or girl, and their weight; then the name of a bear; then a mention of either bud-season or fall-season; and finally a date based on the reign of King Antonius.

'What does it all mean?' asked Benjamin, hoping against hope that Mops or Spike could come up with an innocent explanation.

'I assume,' said Mops, 'these plaques are referring to when the...' she shuddered, 'the things on the wall were...were—'

'Ripped off the humans who were wearing them!' said Spike brutally. 'Come on, it's obvious what those words mean. There's no point pretending otherwise.'

Mops stiffened. 'You're right, Spike,' she said, her voice thick with sorrow. 'We've got to face it. These clothes belonged to humans who were caught by bears...'

'And ripped to shreds,' said Benjamin grimly. 'Or near enough.'

'The plaques say who did it,' said Mops, 'and when. Either in bud-season or fall-season.'

'What I *don't* understand,' said Spike, 'is what they're doing on the wall, hung up for all to see.'

'I agree,' snapped Mops, 'they're hardly something to be proud of!'

Benjamin shook his head. Tears stained his face. There was only one answer to Spike's question as far as he could see; one that spelled the death of every hope he'd ever felt about Hide-Park.

'You're wrong, Mops,' he said softly. 'That's exactly what they are – something those bears *are* proud of.'

'Catching a human?'

'Yes. It must be yet another of the games they play with us, like baiting and betting on sap-fights. Except that this is the worst game of them all. A bear who catches a sap gets the right to put one of these things on the wall.'

'So that's why we're in here,' said Spike, slowly. 'That's why Bearon Weimar's being kind to us and feeding us. So him and his friends can turn up some time and enjoy the fun of chasing us – and ripping us to bits when they catch us. That's what 'hunted-by' must mean.'

'Surely not,' retorted Mops. 'I mean, how much of a challenge would it be to chase and catch somebody like Belinda Dump—' She stopped, gasping in horror as she remembered what Belinda had told them. 'When Bearon Weimar bought Belinda he told her owner that "she'd give them a run-easy"!'

'That's exactly *why* she's here, Mops,' said Benjamin. 'To give even the most useless hunting-bears somebody they can catch!'

'And what did Bearon Weimar say about Mary Graceful when he bought her?' asked Spike. 'He said, "will-she us-give a run-good for money-our!" I'm right about what 'hunted-by' means, you know I am.'

Benjamin nodded grimly. 'You must be, Spike.' Even as he said it, though, Benjamin was searching desperately for a glimmer of hope. 'Maybe it's not going to happen soon. Maybe we'll have a chance to make plans.'

But Spike shook his head. 'Them plaques only mention two times: bud-season and fall-season.'

Bud-season: when buds begin to break out into young green leaves. And fall-season: when those same leaves turn into glorious hues of gold and red and orange before fluttering to the ground – as they were now.

'We're *in* fall-season,' said Benjamin, hopelessly.

'And we won't see bud-season!' cried Mops.

'And none of those who came here last bud-season are still around,' said Spike. '*That's* why nobody's been here more than six moons. Those bears always carry on with their sap-hunting till the very end – till there's nobody left.'

Mops looked down at her own pink clothes, still looking good from her time being pampered by Queen Dearie in Bearkingdom-Palace.

'Well, if they think they're going to stick these up on this wall with a plaque saying which disgusting bear ripped them to shreds then they've got another think coming!' she raged.

Spike's grim face softened, then broke into a grin. 'Well said, Squawker!' He looked down at his own rather grubby outfit. 'Same goes for these!' He turned to Benjamin with a determined look on his face. 'Come on, matey. We need one of your ideas. What are we going to do?'

'Keep going?' suggested Mops.

'As far as that lake?' added Spike. 'See if there's a way out up there?'

Benjamin shook his head. 'No,' he sighed. 'We've got to go back.'

'Go back!' cried Mops. 'Are you mad, Benjamin Wildfire? What in Bear Kingdom do we want to go back for?'

'To warn the others,' said Benjamin simply. 'They think that Bearon Weimar and Inspector Dictatum turned up just looking for us. But they're after everybody. That's why we've got to go back − to warn them...'

The words died on his lips as they heard, coming from the main chamber outside, the steady click

117

click sound of something moving slowly across the wooden floor.

Paw-steps?

His heart pounding, Benjamin shrank back against the wall. Alongside him, Mops and Spike did the same. To spot them, a bear would have to come right in to the room where they were. Perhaps they would be lucky.

But now the steps were coming closer, each one making its clicking, claw-like sound on the wooden floor. Benjamin tensed, ready to leap out and hammer his head into any furry stomach that came round the corner. With luck, the attack would cause such a surprise they'd have time to reach the window and get away.

Still the claw-steps came nearer. Clickety-click. Clickety-click.

And then a low voice hissed, 'Benjamin, where are you? It's me, Roger Broadback.'

ROGER'S RETURN

Roger's appearance was greeted with great joy. With much relief too, at discovering he wasn't a bear, and that the claw-like sounds had been made by the curious nailed boots on his feet. Even so, after the hugs and handshakes, Benjamin insisted that they leave the lodge at once, before Bearon Weimar or any other real bear turned up.

Helping each other out through the window, they hurried back into the safety of the surrounding forest. There they followed their beaten track back to the tulip-tree. Only then, and with eight watchful eyes open for the slightest sign of company, did they settle down to exchange news.

It was, without exception, all bad.

Benjamin, of course, wanted to know what news there was of his father and mother. Roger recounted what had happened at Bearon Weimar's den, and of how all three had been captured by Inspector Dictatum's surprise return.

'So that's what he was doing with Bearon Weimar,'

said Mops. 'We saw them arrive. That's why we ran. But why were they *here*?'

Roger looked at the already miserable Benjamin and sighed. 'Bearon Weimar's daughter-cub told them she'd seen you here, Benjamin. They came to make sure. You see…Inspector Dictatum has suggested that the bearon captures you.'

'For revenge, matey,' growled Spike.

'No,' said Roger to Benjamin. 'To put you with your parents to make a hair-red family he could give to King Bruno as a present. He thinks that would guarantee him the job of Chancellor.'

Mops smiled weakly. 'At least the three of you would be together again.'

'As never-moves,' said Spike grimly. 'What else would the new king do with a hair-red family?'

Benjamin couldn't even begin to think about whether or not that was a price worth paying. Something was confusing him. 'If my mother and father are still locked up at Bearon Weimar's den,' he asked Roger, 'how did you manage to get away?'

Roger Broadback lifted his feet to show them his nailed boots. 'Cart-sap's boots,' he said. 'They put me in a team of ten and chained us to the front of Bearon Weimar's travel-cart. Coming out here was my first journey. I thought it was going to be my last. It was even worse than being a galley-sap.'

Mops drummed her fingers impatiently. 'Do you

mind saving the details for later, Roger? Just answer Benjamin's question.'

'Right,' continued Roger quickly. 'Well, when we arrived we were all so exhausted that the driver unchained us and passed round a bucket of water. Suddenly I heard Bearon Weimar's daughter-cub squeal. I turned round and just caught sight of the three of you running towards the trees. Then I spotted that tree-trunk bridge. So before anybody could stop me, I jumped up and ran across it.'

'And I bet you weren't followed,' said Benjamin.

'No. When I got across the bridge I dived out of sight and kept watch. If any bear *had* come after me, I'd have given myself up rather than put you all in any danger. But when the cart-driver told Bearon Weimar what I'd done, he didn't seem to get angry or anything. He just shrugged. I stayed watching them until they drove off. That's when I followed the path and found the glade. You'd left by then, but luckily I met a boy with a strange name.'

'Only Armstrong, by any chance?' smiled Mops.

'That's right! He showed me the way you'd gone. I set off across that chasing-field but it soon got too dark to see where I was going. So I just flopped down and fell asleep. I was so exhausted from that cart-sap run that I didn't wake up till after sun-come. Finding a freshly-trodden path through the forest was the clue I needed to which way you'd gone. I followed it – and you know the rest.' As he finished his story, something that Benjamin had said came to mind. 'You said you bet I wasn't followed. Why?'

'For the same reason Bearon Weimar shrugged after you'd run over the bridge,' said Benjamin grimly. 'He knew they'd be coming back to search for you soon enough.' He then broke the awful news. 'Roger, this isn't the wonderful place we thought it was. It's a place where humans are hunted!'

They described the awful trophies they'd been looking at in the lodge before Roger's arrival. Then Benjamin leapt to his feet, bristling with urgency. 'Come on, everybody. We've got to get out of this place. We've got to warn the others, then get moving.'

'Where?' asked Roger.

'Anywhere, matey. There's got to be *somewhere*.'

'Bearon Weimar's den,' said Mops quietly. She shrugged as the others looked at her in amazement. 'It's obvious. He can't be in two places at the same time, can he? When he comes back here, he won't be there. Roger knows the way to his den. So he takes us to it, we wait until the bears leave for their disgusting sap-hunting, we rescue Benjamin's parents and then – oh, I don't know, I'm sure we'll think of something when the time comes.'

'Squawker,' said Spike admiringly, 'I don't know how you do it.'

'Talent,' shrugged Mops with a smile. 'Nothing more, nothing less.'

Their plan formulated, they raced back across the chasing-field. Spike had suggested waiting until dark, but Benjamin had convinced him that it wouldn't matter if they were spotted: they were safe until the sap-hunt began, whenever that was. And so they ran and ran, until finally they plunged through the trees and into the glade. They found the others gathered silently about the food hopper. It was almost empty.

'They didn't bring us any food,' said Only Armstrong dully. 'But they *couldn't* have forgotten us. They were all still here after sun-go. We heard their growl-cheering.' His frown deepened further. 'And why have you lot come back?'

Before anyone could answer, Mary Graceful pointed at the water barrel. Its tap was fully open, but no more than a few drops were coming out. 'They didn't bring any water either,' she cried. 'Why not?'

Benjamin was in no doubt. If the bears had stopped providing food and water, it could mean only one thing: that they no longer had any reason to keep them alive and well. The sap-hunt was due to begin.

Leaving Mops and Roger Broadback to tell the others their awful news, Benjamin and Spike hurried away along the path beneath the tunnel of trees which led to the bridge across the chasm.

'We've got to get away before sun-come,' muttered

Benjamin as they ran along the final stretch. 'We can't leave it any later than that.'

Suddenly, Spike stopped. 'We can't get away at all, matey,' he said with a groan.

The bridge was no longer there.

THE OPENING-CEREMONY

Bearon Weimar had supervised the removal of the Hide-Park bridge. It had taken place the previous sun-go and had been the cause of the growl-cheering that Only Armstrong and the others had heard.

It was a ceremony he never missed. That was why he hadn't gone back to his own den, ten thousand paw-paces away (which was what Roger Broadback had assumed). Instead he'd gone to the nearby den of a bear named Petrifus to find out how he'd been getting on with an important job Bearon Weimar had given him. Then, just before sun-go, he'd returned to Hide-Park for the Opening-Ceremony.

By then, the whole area leading to the bridge had been strung with tiny, twinkling torch-lights. The spectator-bears who had been spread throughout the hummock-dotted valley side during light-time were now packed closely together. Cubs sat on their fathers' shoulders. The air was so heavy with excitement it could have been cut with a claw.

Bearon Weimar had padded to the very foot of

the three-trunk bridge. There he gave a short speech.

'Pleasure-much has-it me-given to organise event-forthcoming!' he boomed. 'Gratified-me many-lots spectator-bears here-present! Certain-me-am will-you rewarded-be with more-lots sights-entertaining!'

This speech was greeted with a burst of growl-cheering, quickly followed by another as Bearon Weimar shouted. 'Forward-step bridge-bears!'

Out from the crowd stepped a trio of bears, all beaming with pride. To be selected as a bridge-bear was an honour.

To much growl-cheering, the bridge-bears began their work. One loped across to the far side and with one slash of his claws cut through the vine-ropes lashing the three trunks together. The other two bridge-bears now joined him. Taking one trunk apiece, they proceeded to wind new, far longer vine-ropes around their ends – a task calling for considerable strength, since each had to support the heavy tree trunk with one paw while winding the vine-rope around it with the other.

This done, the bridge-bears then hurried carefully back across the chasm clutching the ends of their vine-ropes.

Bearon Weimar drew himself up to his full height. He raised a four-clawed paw. 'Ready-you? Steady-you?' he roared – then with a cutting motion brought his paw swiftly down. 'Heave-you!'

Each of the three bridge-bears immediately dug his rear claws hard into the base of his trunk to stop it from moving. Then, with roars of effort, they each leaned back and began to pull on their vine-ropes. Slowly the far ends of the three trunks began to rise. The bridge-bears roared louder, digging their claws ever-deeper into the wood to avoid the disgrace of letting their tree trunk topple into the chasm. More than once a bridge-bear yelped with pain as the strain on his claws grew greater. When this happened, Bearon Weimar roared, 'Not-you-be baby-cub! Pain-ignore!'

And the bridge-bears did as they were told, for they all knew the story of how, in his younger days, Bearon Weimar had himself been selected as a bridge-bear and not uttered a single yelp, even though he'd damaged one of his claws so badly that it later fell out.

Little by little the three trunks rose, as if the bridge was being lifted to allow a galley-float to sail underneath. Then they were vertical, as straight and proud as when they were growing. By now the hard work for the bridge-bears was over. Having released their rear claws, they'd backed away as they'd pulled their trunk higher. Now came the moment they would boast about to their cubs – and their cub's cubs – for ever more.

As the whole mass of bear-spectators roared, 'Timber-topple!' they gave a final jerk on their vine-ropes to bring their trunks crashing down to the ground. Bearon Weimar now stepped forward. Leaping on to the middle of the three trunks, he turned to the crowd and made the formal announcement, 'Declare-me official-begun the Hide-Park Sap-Hunt!'

After this, Bearon Weimar, Filia his daughter-cub, and Inspector Dictatum (his now-trusted adviser) had travelled the ten thousand paw-paces back home to Bearon Weimar's den. On this occasion, he didn't order his cart-saps to be flogged too hard. For one thing, after Roger Broadback's escape, they were a cart-sap short. Silly sap. He would come to regret his decision. The agonies of being a cart-sap were nothing to those he would suffer in Hide-Park!

A second reason for taking things more slowly than usual was that in three sun-comes' time they would be travelling back to Hide-Park again for the sap-hunt. The last thing he would want then was the irritation of being slowed down through having a cart-sap drop dead through exhaustion. Giving them a bit of a rest on this journey seemed a good idea. Even so, having left Hide-Park just before middle-night, they had completed the journey along the quiet cart-way by the time the first hint of sun-come was lightening the sky.

Bearon Weimar had slept most of the way, Filia curled up tight beside him. He woke in an even more cheerful mood than when he'd nodded off. He was looking forward to the sap-hunt very much. He was especially going to enjoy hunting the Benjamin-sap. But what he was looking forward to more than anything else was handing over the Benjamin-sap and his hair-red parents to the new King Bruno – and being rewarded with the job of Chancellor in return. So confident was Bearon Weimar that this was what would happen, he could almost feel the new chain of office around his neck.

He lifted Filia gently from the travel-cart, only to have his daughter-cub wake with a question on her lips.

'Can-me hunt-watch, Papa? Please!'

Bearon Weimar smiled. To many, many other bears it would have been seen as a cold, cruel smile. To Filia it was a father-bear's loving smile.

'Promise-me *go*-you-will, daughter-my...' he said – and Filia couldn't talk-sweet him into saying any more than that, however hard she tried.

It wasn't long before the first of Bearon Weimar's hunting guests began to arrive. Invited by the wily bearon in return for a favour or three, they too were looking forward to a thrilling time. The sap-hunt was the high point of the sporting calendar. Over the next couple of sun-comes further guests swelled the numbers, all making temporary dens in the bearon's large grounds. The last of them arrived by torch-light, long after the third sun-go following the Hide-Park bridge opening ceremony.

'Leave-we at dawn-crack,' said Bearon Weimar to Inspector Dictatum.

'Be-me waiting-ready,' growled the Inspector.

Bearon Weimar lowered his voice. 'Want-you me-help out-sniff the hair-red, Inspector. Want-me-not him-caught by other-any.'

'Will-it pleasure-be,' said Inspector Dictatum silkily. 'Er...Bearon Weimar...' The great bear paused, his slow brain trying to work out how best to put the question, '...do-you-what with hair-reds already-caught?'

'Mean-you never-move and husband-her?' said Bearon Weimar. 'Here-them-leave. Have-they hands-feet up-chained. Will-be Forthold them-guarding. They nowhere-go.'

This wasn't the answer Inspector Dictatum wanted. 'Not-think-you...them-take to Hide-Park?'

Bearon Weimar snorted. 'For-why? Them-me-have already-caught! No. Will catch-me the Benjamin-sap and here-him-bring.' The bearon gave a little sigh of sorrow. There was only one disappointment to him about the whole plan. 'Must remember-me to claw-gentle. King Bruno will want-not a sap-scarred.'

Inspector Dictatum didn't argue any further. He would have liked to kill all three saps with one stone, but if he had to tear them to shreds separately then so be it. He would help Bearon Weimar catch his hair-red. But if he, Inspector Dictatum, had anything to do with it, then by the time Benjamin Wildfire had been caught he was going to be a very scarred sap indeed.

After a dry, crisp dark-time, the grounds surrounding Bearon Weimar's den rang with the excited growl-chatter of bears ready to hunt. Gathered together at the bearon's front door, they looked an impressive sight. Black-furred or brown, grey-furred or silver, each wore a scarlet sash round their middle. This wasn't just for show. It was so that the saps could see them coming and become increasingly terrified as they drew nearer.

When every bear was present, the front door opened and out padded Forthold with goblets of root-rum for the ceremonial starting drink. Bearon Weimar raised his goblet to one and all.

'Hunting-good!' he bellowed. 'Hunting-good!' echoed the reply.

Quickly the hunting-bears downed their drinks and began to board their various travelling-carts. Filia, almost bursting with the excitement of it all, ran up to her father's travel-cart, all ready to jump up between him and Lady Weimar. Bearon Weimar shook his head. 'Sorry-me, Filia. Come-you-not us-with.'

'Oh, Papa!' she wailed. 'Promised-you-me!'

Bearon Weimar growl-chuckled at his little trick. 'Never-me promise-break you-to, daughter-my!' (Which was true. He'd often broken promises to others, but *never* to her). He pointed. 'Come-you-not us-with...because go-you *them*-with,' he pointed.

A second travel-cart had just pulled up nearby. Not only was it already occupied by a number of younger bears, also wearing yellow sashes, it was also laden with a variety of weaponry. Filia could see solid cruncheons, viciously barbed spike-poles, sharp-pointed throwing-sticks and much, much more.

Filia's eyes opened wide. 'Mean-you...Filia-be... sap-scarer?'

Bearon Weimar nodded. 'Am-you enough-old,' he said, handing his delighted daughter-cub a yellow sash to put on. 'Petrifus leader-is. When visited-we den-his, ordered-me Petrifus to after-you-look.'

He bent low, until they were snout-to-snout. 'And forget-not, Filia. Job-your is saps-make terror-scared. Way-that, run-them into sap-traps!'

SAP-SCARERS

Benjamin, Mops, Spike and Roger Broadback were already very frightened. Since discovering that the bridge had been removed, nothing had happened to make them feel at all hopeful of escaping what they now knew was to come.

Benjamin and Spike rushed back and told the others that the bridge had gone. By then, Roger and Mops had told them all about the gruesome exhibits in the hunting-lodge. They'd gone through all the other facts which proved that Hide-Park wasn't a haven for saps but a hunting-ground: that nobody there had arrived before bud-season, the time of the previous sap-hunt; that so many of them had been bought by Bearon Weimar; and, finally, that the sudden lack of food and drink meant the bears were no longer worried about keeping them fit and healthy.

'Why go to the bother of feeding us if they're about to tear us to bits,' Spike had said bluntly.

Then Benjamin announced that he, Mops, Spike and Roger had decided to leave their cabins first thing the following sun-come.

'Who wants to come with us?' he asked.

Only Armstrong put up his hand. 'Me. I'm convinced.'

Penelope Curls, the girl they'd seen brought to Hide-Park in a sack, raised her hand. 'Me,' she said, before yanking up the hand of an undecided Oliver Spindle and adding, 'Him too.'

Others followed. But, by the time all the hands stopped moving, still not many more than half were raised.

'I'm staying put,' said Belinda Dumpling. 'You didn't believe my story about there being bears in them woods and I don't believe yours. I've been well-fed here, thank you very much, and I'm going nowhere.' She gave a satisfied smile. 'I'm sure they've just forgotten the food today. If you go it means more for me when they *do* bring it.'

Mary Graceful was on Belinda Dumpling's side. 'It's really nice here. I've never been happier anywhere. I'm staying too.'

There were quite a few nods of agreement, some of them from those who'd already changed their minds after saying they were going to leave with Benjamin. He despaired for them, but realised that there was little more he could do.

And so, finally, they'd all gone back to their cabins to sleep if they were staying or to get ready if they were leaving. Not that there was much *to* get ready. The food supplied by the bears had been so plentiful and regular that none of them had thought of stocking up for emergencies such as this.

'We'll find enough to eat in the forest,' said Benjamin optimistically. 'And I bet there are lots of fish in that lake.'

'If we get that far,' said Spike and Roger, almost at the same time.

Mops stamped her foot in irritation. 'Of course we'll get there! Benjamin got us out of the Howling-Tower, didn't he? And he got us out of Bearkingdom-Palace, didn't he? So getting us out of this place is going to be *perfectly* simple!' She looked imploringly at Benjamin. 'Isn't it?'

'If we stick together it will be,' said Benjamin, remembering what his father had said to him just before they'd parted: 'Son, with friends like these I know you won't fail.'

And so, early next sun-come, they left the comfort of their cosy cabins and set off. As they emerged from the trees and into the chasing-field, a burst of growl-cheers carried faintly across to them from the hillside beyond the chasm. On and around the hummocks a scattering of bears were watching – and waiting, from the look of the makeshift dens of branches and earth that many of them had constructed.

Benjamin took heart from this. 'Maybe the hunters won't be coming for a while,' he said. 'Those bears wouldn't have bothered making dens otherwise.'

'Why are they here at all, then?' asked Mops.

'To get the best view?' said Roger

Mops was appalled. 'You mean they're going to watch us being chased and ripped apart? I can't believe any bear would enjoy that.'

'You would if you'd been in a fighting-pit, Squawker,' said Spike. 'They love it.'

'Then all the more reason for Benjamin to get his thinking cap on,' said Mops, hurrying ahead to Benjamin's side. 'Have you had an idea yet?'

Benjamin ducked the question. 'Let's get to the tulip-tree first, eh? Then we can talk about what to do next.'

The growl-cheering subsided into a watchful silence as the group began their trek across the chasing-field. They kept to the very centre, so that they would spot any hunting-bear who tried to cross the chasm towards them – although how they could do that quickly, without a bridge to cross, Benjamin didn't know.

At the head of the column, he and Mops now concentrated on keeping everybody going at a good pace. Having taken up positions at the rear, Spike and Roger were keeping watch for any sign of a hunting-bear bursting out from the trees surrounding the glade. Tense and frightened, Benjamin remembered the day Mops had madly rolled herself onto the flopping-board. Then the chasing-field had made him feel alive and free. Now it seemed exposed and dangerous. He desperately wanted to reach the cover of the forest in the distance.

Once there, he and Mops led the group no further than the tulip-tree. When they stopped, every eye turned expectantly in Benjamin's direction.

'Well, what's the plan?' asked Mops.

It was an awful moment. Benjamin simply didn't *have* a plan. He'd been racking his brains ever since they'd left the glade but nothing had come to him. He had to admit as much.

'Oh,' said Mops, deflated.

'All I know,' said Benjamin, 'is that we can't go back.'

'And we can't go forward either, matey,' said Spike. 'For all we know, them bears could be getting together at that lodge place. We'd walk straight into them.'

'Then it sounds as if we're staying here,' said Roger Broadback.

And, as Benjamin thought about it, staying where they were didn't seem that bad a thing to do.

'We can take turns to keep watch on the chasing-field,' said Benjamin, 'while the rest of us can try to make shelters out of branches.' He looked around. Being fall-season, the nut-bushes were laden with nuts. 'And gather food,' he said, trying to be as bright as possible.

The others nodded, but without enthusiasm. 'Good idea,' said Only Armstrong, flatly.

And so, for the next two sun-comes — while Bearon Weimar's hunting-party were gathering excitedly — the frightened humans stayed in hiding, never venturing far from each other and the tulip-tree. For his part, Benjamin ignored how hungry and thirsty he was becoming and spent every available moment trying to think of a way to escape from the hunting-bears. But still nothing came. As sun-come followed sun-come, the humans who'd left their comfortable cabins to follow Benjamin were growing increasingly restless.

'Nothing,' said Penelope Curls, returning from keeping watch on the chasing-field. 'Not a hunting-bear to be seen. Just more and more bears lolling on the hummocks, that's all.'

'Like they did before,' complained Oliver Spindle. 'None of them came over the chasm then, and I don't think they're going to do it now.'

Some of the others nodded in agreement. 'I reckon we should go back,' said one. 'I'm missing my bed.'

'No, don't do it!' cried Benjamin.

But the revolt grew quickly. Nods were exchanged. People scrambled to their feet. In next to no time, Penelope Curls was leading a grumbling group the short distance from the tulip-tree to where the chasing-field began. Painfully, Benjamin watched them go...and saw them stop. An instant later they were running back, sheer terror in their eyes.

'They're here!' screamed Penelope, 'they're here!'

Benjamin and the others raced to the edge of the forest and looked out. Having left his den at the crack of sun-come, Bearon Weimar's hunting-party had arrived. To an excited burst of growl-cheering from the hordes of spectator-bears, the party clattered to a halt at the open space close to where the bridge had been.

The hunting-bears jumped down at once, their yellow and crimson sashes clearly visible. A number of them immediately loped across to where the three huge tree trunks, which had made the bridge across the chasm, still lay after the opening-ceremony. Working in teams, the hunting-bears then hoisted these trunks on to their broad shoulders. Followed by the remainder of the hunting-party, and accompanied by the rhythmic paw-pounding of the spectator-bears, the three teams carried these trunks to a point, Benjamin judged, not far beyond where the flopping-board was. There the trunks were hoisted upright, then pushed forward so that their ends landed on the other side of the chasm with three great thuds. Before the dust had even settled, the bears of the hunting-party were swarming across these makeshift bridges, their sharp claws keeping them perfectly balanced as they moved.

'Get ready to run if they come this way!' said Benjamin loudly, his voice quivering with fear.

But none of the bears *were* coming their way. In fact, only some of them were moving at all. Having crossed the chasm, the red-sashed bears had padded just the few paw-paces to the edge of the chasing-field then settled down. It was those with yellow sashes round their middles who were on the move. They were heading towards the trees surrounding the glade. Amongst them, though too far away for either Benjamin, Mops or Spike to recognise her, was Filia Weimar...

Filia was more excited than she'd even been in her young life. Petrifus, the sap-scarer's leader, had met the cavalcade as it passed his den. He was a wizened old bear who was no longer quick enough on his legs to be a sap-hunter. During the remainder of their journey to Hide-Park he'd explained what would happen and how important the sap-scarer's job was to the success of the hunt. Filia had listened carefully and was determined to do her job well.

Moving stealthily to the edge of the glade, she crouched down behind a red-berried prickle-bush and waited for Petrifus to give his signal. Filia could see him moving stiffly into position on the far side of the glade. He, in turn, would be waiting for the sap-scarers to completely surround the sap-cabins and then...

'Sap-scare!'

Petrifus's howl-cry came so suddenly it took Filia by surprise. Before she'd even moved, the other yellow-sashed sap-scarers were pouring into the glade. Some yanked open cabin doors before scampering round and round the outsides, thumping loudly on the walls. Others climbed onto the roofs and hammered on them with their cruncheons. Whatever they did, every sap-scarer accompanied their activity with the most frightening roar they could manage.

Filia had been armed with a spike-pole – a pole about twice her length, claw-sharpened to give it a wickedly pointed end. Scampering into the glade to join the fun, she found that terrified saps had already begun to run screaming from their cabins. The sap-scarers now began to howl and roar, 'Way-that! Way-that!', jabbing and hitting the saps so as to force them along the narrow track which led out to the chasing-field. Petrifus ordered a couple of the sap-scarers to begin checking the cabins for hiding-saps.

For a moment, Filia felt bitter disappointment. Was that going to be all that was left for her to do? Then, out from the nearest cabin came a large, round grown-older (Belinda Dumpling, though of course Filia wasn't to know who she was). She was screaming. Her hands were waving and her whole body was wobbling with fright. This was her chance! Scampering forward, Filia jabbed at Belinda Dumpling with her spike-pole and scored a direct hit in the terrified woman's fleshy upper arm.

'That way!' shouted Filia in human-talk. 'That way!'

Belinda Dumpling looked around wildly, not knowing which way to go. The sap-scarers gave her no choice. By now they'd encircled the glade so that – like the neck of a round bottle – the track to the chasing-field was the only way to go. Prompted by another sharp jab from Filia, this time in her round behind, Belinda Dumpling lumbered that way.

'Done-all!' roared Petrifus, the sap-scarer's leader. 'Them-chase!'

A great growl-cheer went up. Beaming delightedly, the sap-scarers now converged on the track and began to hurry along it themselves.

At the rear, her spike-pole tinged with Belinda Dumpling's blood, Filia Weimar gave a growl-cheer of her own. The first part of her job was done – but only the first part. There would be more to come, much more!

So why didn't she feel as madly excited as before? Why hadn't she growl-cheered as wildly as the others? Why did she feel so…odd?

THE CHASING-FIELD

The scarlet-sashed hunting-bears were ready and waiting.

No longer were they lolling around. The moment they'd heard the first sounds of the sap-scarers' work they'd quickly got onto all fours. Now they were tensed and alert, every one of them looking as if they were poised for violent and sudden movement. Their tactics were obvious. By running up the sloping ground on that side of the chasing-field (the same slope that Mops had rolled down with such glee) they wouldn't be seen until they crested its brow. By then they would be going at full speed and not even the fastest human would be able to outrun them.

'Oh no,' gasped Benjamin. 'Here they come.'

Hounded by the sap-scarers, the humans they'd left behind had begun to flood out into the chasing-field. The moment they did, the hunter-bears launched themselves forward. As each scarlet-sashed bear reached the top of the slope, they picked out a human target and began to lumber rapidly after them.

'Oh, no,' moaned Mops. 'That's Mary Graceful.'

The long-legged girl was unmistakeable. Having emerged from the trees, she'd quickly found herself being chased by a fat, brown bear with dripping jaws. They watched as Mary Graceful, clearly stricken with panic, began to run as fast as her slim legs would carry her. Her long hair flowing out behind her, she zig-zagged wildly as the fat bear lumbered in pursuit. For a moment it seemed as if the bear was catching her. Then, suddenly, as if it had completely run out of steam, the bear stopped.

'Yes!' cheered Benjamin, along with everyone else.

But his delight was short-lived. Another scarlet-sashed bear had taken up where the first had left off. This one was fitter and leaner. Loping across the ground, it quickly narrowed the gap between itself and the fleeing Mary Graceful. Desperately she twisted and turned, trying to run but also wanting to see how close the hunting-bear was behind her.

'The chasm!' screamed Mops. 'Watch out!'

Mary Graceful couldn't hear her, of course. Even if she had been able to, it wouldn't have helped. Still racing at top speed, but still looking behind her, the poor girl simply didn't realise how far and in what direction she'd run. As Mary Graceful suddenly disappeared from view, Mops buried her face in her hands and cried inconsolably.

The horror continued. One after another, the terrified humans were chased and caught in a flurry of claws. Some were carried off, screaming. Others, once a hunter had grabbed them, simply didn't get to their feet again.

This was the fate that befell Belinda Dumpling. The last one to reach the chasing-field, the poor grown-older emerged from the trees just as the fat brown bear who'd had to give up chasing Mary Graceful had got his breath back. With his energy renewed, the fat bear gave chase. Belinda didn't have a chance. Desperately she turned and tried to run back into the trees. The fat bear went after her. They both vanished from sight. There was a piercing scream, then nothing – nothing, that is, until the fat bear came back into view, waving a shredded blouse.

From the hummocks beyond the chasm came the cheering of the spectator-bears. But of one sound there came no more – the sound of terrified screaming. The meaning was obvious. Mercifully, Benjamin and the others had been too far away to see the full horror of what had happened. The little they *had* seen had been terrible enough, as had the screams. And now the end of the screaming told them more.

'That's it, isn't it?' said Roger Broadback. 'They're all...' He slumped into silence, unable to say the word.

Benjamin could only nod. They would never again see Belinda Dumpling, Albert Gaptooth, Mary Graceful or any of the others they'd left behind in the glade cabins. The only evidence that they'd ever lived would be a shredded garment hanging on the wall of the trophy-chamber in Bearon Weimar's hunting-lodge.

Mops tried to wipe the tears from her eyes, but still they kept coming. She forced her question out. 'Do you think the bears will go away now?'

Benjamin shook his head, while Spike said, 'No chance, Squawker.'

For, throughout the whole session of sap-chasing, two bears hadn't joined in at all. The unmistakeable figures of Bearon Weimar and, beside him, Inspector Dictatum, hadn't chased or harried or clawed. While all this had been going on around them, they'd remained stock still, just staring at the stream of terrified humans being chased out by the sap-scarers.

'Why aren't they joining in?' Benjamin had asked.

'Why d'you think?' Spike had replied. 'They're waiting for *you* to come out.'

Much as he wanted to believe otherwise, Benjamin knew this was true. Bearon Weimar wanted him and no other. Even worse, he'd recruited Inspector Dictatum to help him.

Now Mops's question about whether it was all over was answered. For away in the centre of the chasing-field, Bearon Weimar and Inspector Dictatum were conferring. As Benjamin watched, the two bears turned in the direction of the forest. Although he knew they couldn't see him, Benjamin felt as if those four eyes were looking right at him. Then he saw Bearon

Weimar and Inspector Dictatum nodding decisively.

At a curt signal from Bearon Weimar, the yellow-sashed sap-scarers now scurried forward to form a straight line, strung out across the centre of the chasing-field. This done, the red-sashed hunting-bears gathered behind them, as if the sap-scarers were forming a protective shield.

Bearon Weimar waited until the lines were formed to his satisfaction. Then, in a voice that carried all the way to where Benjamin and the others were hiding, he roared, 'To the Hunting-Forest!'

And they began, slowly and steadily, to march their way.

THE HUNTING-FOREST

There was no talk of going back to the cabins now, just gratitude to Benjamin for having saved them from the horror of what they'd just seen and heard.

'That would have happened to us if we'd stayed behind,' said an ashen-faced Only Armstrong. Penelope Curls, Oliver Spindle and the others who had left the cabins with them nodded in agreement.

'Or if you'd gone back, as you were about to,' said Mops sharply.

Nobody needed telling. One glance out towards the sap-scarers slowly – very slowly – coming their way, was sufficient reminder of that. It also told them that they could stay where they were no longer. Instinctively, everybody in the group turned to Benjamin.

'We have no choice now,' he said. 'We've got to stay out of sight. So we're going to have to head on further into the forest.'

The *Hunting*-Forest, he thought. That's what Bearon Weimar had just growl-shouted to the others. Why? Was it a cruel name he'd just thought up, or was there

148

more to it than that? But there was no time to think about an answer. They had to move quickly. With Roger Broadback leading the way, the whole group raced back to the tulip-tree.

'Now what?' he asked when they got there.

'Do we have any choice?' said Mops. She pointed along the beaten track which led to Bearon Weimar's hunting-lodge. 'We'd be mad to go that way. Any time now that lodge is going to be crawling with bears wanting to hang up their disgusting trophies.'

Shuddering at the thought, Benjamin didn't even stop moving. Veering past the tulip-tree, he led the group on to the path that Filia Weimar had taken after he'd saved her.

'This is risky, matey,' said Spike, hurrying to catch him up.

'I know,' said Benjamin. 'I'm just hoping that *all* the hunting-bears are following us. If they are, then it means there won't be any in *front* of us.'

And, as they hurried on, it seemed as though Benjamin's reasoning was correct. They'd heard the occasional growl-call from far behind them, but seen no sign of any activity ahead. What was more, the path they were following had turned out to be flat and open. It curved gently this way and that, so that Benjamin sometimes wasn't certain whether they were heading up towards the lake at the top of Hide-Park, or in a more sideways direction towards the parts of the chasing-field which skirted both sides of the forest. He decided that it didn't much matter. The important thing was that the path had been clear enough to allow the whole group to move quickly, even the younger ones like Oliver Spindle. He'd occasionally shouted, 'Don't go so fast!' but with Penelope Curls's encouragement – and the occasional piggyback from Roger – he'd been able to keep up.

The forest was beautiful. Sometimes they found themselves plunging through a dense cluster of trees, at others through small glades carpeted with golden leaves.

It was at just such a spot that they found the food hopper. It was full to overflowing. Delicious smells were wafting from it. Mops, who by then had hurried forward to join Benjamin at the head of the group, slowed instantly.

'Ignore it, Mops,' called Benjamin. 'We haven't got time.'

But Mops now came to a complete halt. 'Benjamin, I haven't eaten since last sun-go.'

'None of us have,' said Penelope, also stopping.

'None of *me* has,' said Oliver Spindle, wriggling down from Roger's back and scurrying to Penelope's side.

One by one the whole group either came to a halt or turned back to where Mops was still staring at the food hopper from the edge of the path.

'Those hunting-bears were moving very slowly,

Benjamin,' Roger Broadback said quietly. 'We must be a good bit ahead of them by now. Maybe we *should* take the chance to eat. We might not get another for a while.'

'Precisely!' cried Mops. 'And what we don't eat we can take with us! Remind me,' she said to Penelope and Oliver as they scurried to her side, 'to tell you about a wonderful wheely-box I used to own. Such capacity...'

Mops didn't finish her sentence. She, Penelope and Oliver had taken no more than a couple of steps towards the hopper when the leaf-covered ground suddenly gave way beneath their feet. With wails of terror, the three of them disappeared from sight.

'It's a trap!' screamed Benjamin.

But he was too late. Seeing Mops make a move, a few of those at the back of the group had begun to push their way towards the hopper from a different direction. With a succession of loud cracks, they too vanished below ground in a shower of leaves and splintered branches.

It all happened so fast that only Spike had managed to react quickly enough to try and help. As the earth opened up in front of little Oliver Spindle, Spike leapt forward to grab him by the back of his shirt. But, strong as he was, even Spike hadn't been able to save him. Worse: as Oliver fell, Spike lost his balance. Moments later, he too was tumbling downwards to land with a thud on the muddy bottom of the bear's sap-trap of a hole.

For that's what it was: a devious trap, the product of Bearon Weimar's devious mind. The claw-dug hole was large and circular, but with a solid centre to support the tempting food hopper. It was deep, too. As Benjamin fell to his knees and crawled to the edge of the hole he found that Mops, Spike, Penelope, Oliver and the others were way below him.

'Can you climb out?' he shouted.

'No chance, matey,' called Spike. 'You'll have to get something to pull us up with.'

'Vines!' said Roger Broadback at once. 'That dense part of the forest we passed through had lots of them.'

Benjamin remembered them. Thick and tough-looking, there had been lots dangling down from the trees. If they were strong enough, they could do the trick!

'Hurry then, Roger!' he shouted. 'Take Only with you. I'll stay here!'

Even as he shouted, Benjamin realised that nobody other than Roger, Only and himself were there. The remainder of the group, on seeing Mops and the others fall into the trap, had panicked and scattered wildly in all directions.

As Roger and Only headed back down the path to search for suitable vines, Benjamin looked again over the lip of the sap-trap hole. There was some movement going on. Penelope and Oliver were scrambling on their hands and knees towards — what? Penelope's excited cry explained it all.

'There's a way out!'

The others in the hole now scrambled her way. 'Light!' cried one.

'What is it, Mops?' shouted Benjamin.

Mops was at the back of the excited throng. 'It looks like this isn't just a hole,' she called up. 'There's a kind of tunnel leading away from it.' Squeezing herself closer, she now saw what Penelope and Oliver had seen. 'It slopes upwards. And there's light at the end of it!'

Desperately, the others in the sap-trap began pushing and shoving for a look. Only Spike stayed back. 'A way *out* of a trap?' he said suspiciously. 'I don't like it.'

'Oh, what do you *ever* like!' shouted Mops. 'When we get to the end we can turn round and come straight back here again!'

Spike looked anxiously up at Benjamin. 'Have you got anything to pull us up with yet?'

'Roger and Only have gone to find a length of strong vine,' shouted Benjamin. 'They'll be back soon.'

'Then I'll wait for them...' called Spike firmly, 'and so will Squawker.'

'No, I will not!' screeched Mops, feeling her arms gripped tight. 'Let me go! Let me go!'

But Spike wouldn't listen. Dragging Mops away, he shouted at Penelope to come back. She, in turn, didn't listen to him. Ducking down, she began to crawl through the tunnel towards the light at the end.

'It's part of the trap!' Spike shouted again and again, as Oliver and the others jostled their way through the tunnel's opening to follow Penelope. None of them turned back.

Only Mops remained, against her will. She struggled and fought, trying to escape from Spike's powerful grip with all her might. She kicked his shins. She called him names (and Mops seemed to know a surprisingly high number). None of it made the slightest difference. Spike continued to hold her tight while pleading with the others to come back.

'Well, I hope you're proud of yourself!' spat Mops when Spike finally released her, only to stand guard at the tunnel entrance so that there was no way for her to get past him. 'When those hunting-bears arrive and pull us out of their trap I trust you'll tell them, "I don't like it" before they tear us to shreds!'

Spike shook his head sorrowfully. 'They'll get Penelope and the others first,' he said flatly.

'What?' cried Mops. 'Is there anything between your ears? They're *escaping*!'

Spike didn't reply. Making sure there was no room for Mops to get past, he ducked to look along the length of the tunnel. Mops, accepting that she couldn't move him out of her way without a small army to help her, bent down angrily to see what was happening.

Penelope had reached the far end, her frizzy hair captured in the circle of light. Out she went. The small shape of Oliver Spindle followed. Then, one by one, out went the others until they'd all left and only the circle of light remained.

'There!' snapped Mops. 'And what exactly isn't there to like about that?'

Her question hung only briefly in the air. Then, from beyond the Hunting-Forest, came a scream of terror. It was followed by another, then another, all to a growl-rumbling background of cheering. In the circle of light at the end of the tunnel they briefly saw Penelope's legs flash past. Then another pair of legs – legs of thick brown fur, ending in sharp-clawed paws.

'Oh, no!' gasped Mops. 'It must lead to the part of the chasing-field that goes down the side of the forest!'

Spike couldn't stop the tears coming. They flowed down his face. 'I should have done more to stop them,' he moaned. 'Grabbed them. Got to that opening first and stood in the way. Pulled Penelope back. Shouted louder...'

'You did everything you could, Spike,' cried Mops. 'It was all you could do to stop me...' She staggered back into the centre of the hole, wide-eyed with the realisation of what could have happened to her. 'If you'd let me go with them...I'd—'

Another high-pitched scream from the chasing-field said it all for her. They wouldn't see the others again.

And had it not been for Spike's determination, she'd have suffered the same fate. Mops looked up at her friend, with his shock of hair and ever-grubby neck.

'Thank you,' she said simply.

A long, thick strip of vine suddenly dangled down between them. Over the edge of the hole jutted the faces of Benjamin, Roger and Only Armstrong.

'Grab hold!' yelled Benjamin. 'And let's hope it's strong enough!'

It was. Mops grabbed hold of the vine and walked up the side of the hole as she was pulled to safety. Spike followed, in spite of the length of vine creaking alarmingly as he climbed up. At the top, they quickly told the others how the trap worked.

'So the next time Spike says he doesn't like something...' said Mops, 'Well, remind me not to like it too!'

Benjamin smiled, but briefly. There was no time to lose. The sap-trap delay would have wiped out most of the lead they'd built up. The scarers, and perhaps some of the hunter-bears too, must have gained a lot of ground on them.

'We've got to keep moving,' he said.

'What about the others?' asked Mops. 'Isn't there anything we can do for them?'

Benjamin shook his head. Penelope, Oliver and those who'd foolishly followed the sap-trap tunnel would have already been caught by now. And although those who'd panicked and run off might still be alive, they could be anywhere in the forest. Much as he wanted, it would be madness to look for them. They had to face the awful fact: the only ones left from their party were himself, Mops, Spike, Roger and Only Armstrong.

He gazed further along the path they'd been following before they'd come across the food-hoppers. It looked clear enough, but who knew what danger lay ahead? One thing was certain. There *was* danger behind. They had no choice but to keep going...

Benjamin and the others had been gone from the sap-trap for little more than a slow count of five hundred before the silence they'd left behind was broken by the sounds of growl-whispering and softly padding paws. Along the path came Petrifus, the leader of the sap-scarers, to look with great satisfaction at the collapsed sap-trap.

'Father-yours will delighted-be!' he said to the young cub at his side. 'Did-him job-good! Proud-you-are?'

Filia Weimar nodded. 'Much-very,' she said. But she didn't really feel it.

'Prouder-you-be when trap-we-all!' said Petrifus. He signalled to the other yellow-sashed scarers, strung out in a line across the width of the Hunting-Forest.

'On-we-go!' he growl-called. 'Run-them-can...but away-not-get!'

TRAPPED

With Benjamin at their head, the little band of five survivors plunged on through the Hunting-Forest. And they *were* soon no longer in any doubt that they were the only survivors. Every now and then a terrifying scream had cut through the trees to tell them that somewhere in the forest one of those who'd run away from the sap-trap had been caught.

As they ran, Benjamin racked his brains. Was there any hope of escape? What would happen if and when they did reach the limits of the Hunting-Forest? What was beyond it? The glittering lake, for sure. But would that give them a way of escaping?

'I doubt if I could swim faster than a bear, if that's what you're saying,' called Roger Broadback, after Benjamin had found enough breath to voice his fears as they ran.

'Well, I certainly couldn't,' added Mops. 'I can't swim at all.'

Spike nearly ran off the path as he turned to look at her. 'You can't swim? Not at all?'

'Water is for *drinking*, Spike,' answered Mops, though not unkindly. 'And – if you don't mind me saying so – *washing*. If we'd been meant to swim in the stuff we'd have been born with flippers.'

Benjamin slowed to a halt, almost crying with fear and frustration. 'Then what *can* we do?'

'Hide?' said Spike, before immediately dismissing his own suggestion. 'No good. There's nowhere *to* hide.'

'Turn back?' suggested Roger Broadback. 'I mean, if we could somehow get *through* that line of bears...'

'They'd be going one way and we'd be going the other!' Only Armstrong cried hopefully – only to shake his head as he realised how impossible it would be to get through the line of bears without being caught.

'How about having something to eat?' said Mops.

As the others looked at her in astonishment, she pointed a little way further down the path. A few paces off to the side, in a little clearing, stood a full food hopper. 'Only joking,' said Mops. 'I bet it's another hole-in-the-ground trap.'

Benjamin's eyes lit up as an idea finally struck him. 'I hope so, Mops!' he cried.

He hurried down the path until he was level with the food hopper. Just as before, it was surrounded by branches and leaves. Back then, they'd been so focussed on the food hoppers that none of them had noticed how unnatural the surrounding ground had looked. Now, Benjamin did. The branches looked as if they'd been *arranged*, then covered with leaves. It *had* to be another trap.

Falling to his knees on the path, Benjamin carefully began to probe the ground in the direction of the hopper with his fingers. For a short way he found solid ground beneath the layer of leaves. Then, as he pushed his hand down, it suddenly went straight through. Easing back the twigs and leaves, he peered through the small gap he'd made. It *was* a trap!

'You've had an idea, haven't you?' said Mops, her voice a mixture of excitement and hope.

'Yes, I think so.'

'Benjamin, this is not time to *think* so! Whatever idea you've had, it's one more than any of us. So what is it?'

Benjamin took a deep breath. 'We hide in the sap-trap until the sap-scarers and the hunting-bears have gone past. Then we get out, grab some food and go back the way we came, towards the cabins.'

'And after that?' asked Spike.

'I don't know,' said Benjamin.

Mops sniffed. 'Well...I have to be honest, Benjamin. It's not one of your finest ideas. But as we're hardly snowed under with them it will have to do for now!'

They quickly got to work. While the others carefully widened the gap in the trap's cover until it was large enough to slip through, Benjamin found another strong length of vine. This he looped around the base of a tree near the trap, before running it across to the gap and dropping it through.

'I'll go first, matey,' volunteered Spike.

Standing with his back to the trap, Spike gripped the vine tightly, then lowered himself through the gap. There was a tense silence until he called up, 'I'm at the bottom. This trap's not as deep as the other one.'

Then Benjamin pulled up the vine-rope and Mops went down. Only Armstrong followed, then Roger Broadback. As he pulled the vine up for the final time, Benjamin asked Roger to stand directly beneath the hole. First, though, he quickly brushed a layer of leaves over the vine-rope so that it couldn't be spotted. Only then did Benjamin lower himself into the trap – but not to the bottom. As his feet came down, Roger guided them on to his own shoulders. With his head at the level of the ground above, Benjamin was now able to pull the branches back into place and close the hole he'd made. Only then did he lift his feet from Roger's shoulders and lower himself the rest of the way down.

'I don't know how well I've covered things up,' he said.

Mops smiled brightly. 'I'm sure you've done an absolutely splendid job. And if you haven't,' she pointed at the tunnel entrance close by, a glimmer of light shining its the far end, 'I suppose we can always take our chances by going out that-a-way.'

The distant sound of growl-calls put paid to all further discussion. The sap-scarers were approaching.

Filia Weimar smelled the food hopper before she saw it. Like all bears, even young cubs like her, her sense of smell was better than her eyesight and the fragrance of the berries and fruits in the hopper had been growing stronger with every step. Had this sap-trap worked as well as the last one?

'Father-your pleased-will-be,' said Petrifus, the sap-scarer's leader, from close by. 'The sap-hunt is well-going.'

He'd been sticking close to Filia ever since they'd entered the hunting-forest: so annoyingly close that she was beginning to wonder whether her papa had told the wizened old bear to do just that.

'When finish-it?' she asked.

Petrifus growl-chuckled unpleasantly. 'When saps-all caught-are.'

'Saps-all? Never-do escape-any?'

'Ever-never.'

Filia's earlier feeling of unhappiness was still with her. 'Many-how think-you left-are?' she asked.

'From sap-screams hear-me,' replied Petrifus, 'Many-not! More-no than a full-paw.'

The food hopper was not far ahead. Filia could see it, standing upright just off the paw-path. What she couldn't yet tell was whether or not the sap-trap had been disturbed. For all she knew, the last few remaining saps could be in it...

As they heard the sap-scarers draw close, Benjamin and the others shrank against the muddy, root-laced walls of the trap. It was dark and dank. A small amount of light was filtering in between the layers of branches and leaves up above their heads, but not much. Even with his eyes adjusted to the darkness, Benjamin could only clearly see Mops, who was right beside him. Over on the other side of the trap Spike, Roger and Only Armstrong were dim outlines.

'I only hope they recognise their own traps,' whispered Mops. 'The last thing we want is for one of them to land in here.'

The paw-paces outside were getting louder. Vague, muffled growl-voices came down to them. For a while they were indistinct, but soon became clearer.

'Sap-trap-this disturbed-not,' said an old gravelly voice.

'Mind-never,' said another, much younger voice – a voice that sounded vaguely familiar to Benjamin.

Now the older voice spoke again. 'But if disturbed-not...why smell-me sap-stink?'

Petrifus's snout was twitching. The old bear had helped dig far too many sap-traps to make the mistake of getting too close and falling in himself. He prowled up and down the pathway, then through the saplings and undergrowth which surrounded the trap.

'*Definitely* smell-me sap-stink,' he said.

Filia twitched her own nose. 'Think-me right-you-are,' she said.

Then she left the pathway too and padded across to a nearby tree. She lowered her snout almost to the ground and sniffed around the base of its trunk. Finally she sat down with her back against the tree and shook her head.

'Think-me right-you-are, Petrifus,' she said again. 'But think-me sap-stink fresh-not. Gone-they-have.'

Petrifus glowered. 'Teach-you bear-old to sap-sniff?' he growled. 'Tell-me-you thing-some, lady-young. Sap-hunting been-me before-since born-you!'

Filia shrugged. 'Why-then sap-trap disturbed-not?'

'Know-me-not.' The old bear scratched his muzzle thoughtfully. Although he didn't like to be corrected by a young cub, Filia was an *important* young cub. 'Perhaps right-you-am,' he said finally. And with that he padded back to the pathway.

But Filia didn't move.

While Petrifus had been investigating the sap-trap, the line of yellow-sashed sap-scarers strung out through the hunting-forest had paused. Now, as he shouted at them, 'On-go!' they resumed their forward march.

Still Filia remained where she was, lazing comfortably against the trunk of the tree.

164

'Hear-you, Filia?' said Petrifus. 'On-we-go. On-come, up-get!'

'Tired-me-am, Petrifus,' replied Filia in a young growl-whine. 'Need-me rest-sit.'

Petrifus snorted irritably. The other sap-scarers were already moving on. 'Later-time for rest-sit. Now up-get!'

'No!' cried Filia. 'Stay-me-here. Will-me up-you-catch.'

Old bear Petrifus didn't know what to do. Either he had to call back the sap-scarers or leave Filia behind until she'd had her rest. He didn't want to call back the scarers because that would cause a delay and be sure to annoy Bearon Weimar. He and the other hunting-bears were waiting in the part of the chasing-field that ran alongside the hunting-forest for the remaining saps to be scared out into the open. But then neither did he want to leave Filia behind.

'Father-your me-told after-you-look,' he snapped at Filia. 'And must-me orders-obey. Bearon Weimar important-is.'

At this, Filia stood and stamped her foot angrily. 'And Filia Weimar important-is!' she shouted. 'Is-me daughter-cub of Bearon Weimar! Means-which if wants-me rest-sit then have-me rest-sit!'

Petrifus knew he was beaten. Muttering under his breath, 'Cubs, who have-them-would?' he began to stomp off up the path. 'Follow-you path-this,' he growled. 'Leads-it-soon to forest-out and magic-lake. Wait-you me-for. And not-you long-be!'

Filia sat down again and leaned against the tree. As she waited, she idly toyed with the thick vine she'd noticed while sniffing near it: a vine that had been looped round the base of its trunk. Dangling the vine between her paws, she lifted it gently, smiling to herself as it came up through the leaves and branches between herself and the edge of the sap-trap.

Satisfied that Petrifus and the other sap-scarers were now well out of both sight and sniffing range, Filia rolled onto her feet. Following the trailing length of vine, she padded slowly across to the sap-trap.

'Come out, Benjamin Wildfire,' she said in perfect human. 'I can smell that you are in there.'

THE HOSTAGE

Down in the trap, Benjamin didn't know what to do. They'd all heard Filia's conversation with Petrifus, breathing a huge sigh of relief when he'd gone away. What they'd now expected was that Filia would rest for a while, then scamper off to catch up with Petrifus as she'd promised. But to be told that she knew Benjamin was down there had completely stunned them.

'Don't go out!' hissed Mops. 'Don't you dare move!'

'You heard her,' said Benjamin. 'She knows I'm here.'

'But she doesn't know *we're* here, matey,' murmured Spike.

Benjamin nodded. 'All the more reason for me to go, then,' he said. 'If she calls for help I'll be the only one caught. You'll still have a chance to get away as we planned.'

Roger Broadback hurried to Benjamin's side and gripped him by the shoulder. 'Calling for help is just what she *will* do, Benjamin.'

'She's a bear-cub,' added Only Armstrong. 'She can't be trusted.'

But something told Benjamin that wasn't so. 'She sent that Petrifus bear away,' he said. 'Why'd she do that?' He gripped the end of the vine and pulled it taut. 'I'm going to take a chance,' he said.

And with that he pulled himself up the side wall, through the branches at the top and out of the sap-trap.

Behind him, the other four huddled together. Spike put into words what they were all thinking. 'First hint of trouble and we go up to help him, right?'

'Right.'

They heard Benjamin speak first.

'You *do* talk human, then.'

'Yes,' said Filia.

'And you understand everything we say?'

Filia pulled herself upright. On her hind legs she was just about the same height as Benjamin.

'Not *everything*. I do not always understand everything my father's cart-saps say, perhaps because they are usually so out of breath. But I do understand most things.'

'How? No other bears ever have.'

'I am not sure,' said Filia. 'Perhaps because I am a cub. The voice of a cub is high, like that of a sap. We speak quickly, like a sap.'

'But grown-older bears don't understand us – and they were cubs once.'

Filia wrinkled her snout. 'Perhaps they've forgotten

what it was like to be young,' she said, before adding firmly, 'which is something I will *never* do.'

Benjamin almost laughed. 'You sound like a girl I know,' he said.

'Is she in the sap-trap too?'

'No!' said Benjamin, a bit too quickly. The shock brought his mind back to the seriousness of the situation, though. 'What are you going to do now?' he asked fiercely. 'Call the hunting-bears to come and cut me to ribbons like the others?'

Filia winced. 'No,' she said quietly, 'I am going to save you, just as you saved me.'

'Save me?' said Benjamin bitterly, the awful screams of those who'd been hunted down still ringing in his ears. 'And how are you going to do that? You know what Hide-Park is for.'

'I am Filia Weimar,' said the young cub matter-of-factly. 'My papa is Bearon Weimar, whose word is law in this place. I will tell him how you saved me when I was at the top of the tree, and ask him to let you go free.'

Benjamin's hopes rose. Filia seemed so confident of herself. Could it be that she really did have that much influence over Bearon Weimar?

'How about my friends?'

Filia smiled knowingly. 'Your friends who my snout tells me are also in the sap-trap?'

Benjamin didn't know what to say. Should he admit she was right? He didn't have to. Hearing a sudden rustling of branches, Benjamin turned to see Mops's head poke out from the sap-trap, followed by the rest of her body as Spike pushed her up. Within a few moments Roger Broadback, then Only Armstrong, then finally Spike himself, clambered up the vine-rope and out of the hole. Filia looked at them all in surprise.

'Four friends? I was expecting two. I am not sure my papa will allow so many to go free.'

'It's not just them,' Benjamin said grimly. 'There's also my mother and father – who have been locked up by *your* father!'

Filia, who had been slowly shaking her head, now shook it furiously. 'That is too much to ask!' she cried. 'I cannot ask my papa for as much as that. You will have to choose: your mother and father – or your friends.'

'But that's not fair!' shouted Benjamin.

Filia frowned. 'Fair? What is 'fair'? I have never heard this word.'

The young cub didn't receive an answer – not then, anyway. For, in a blur of movement, Spike charged across and grabbed her from behind. Pinning Filia's arms to her sides he yelled at Only Armstrong to grab the vine-rope that Spike had pulled up behind him when he'd emerged from the sap-trap.

'What are you doing?' yelled Benjamin.

'Taking a hostage, matey, that's what! That bearon might not want to let us all go but if he thinks it's the only way to save his daughter-cub then it could change his mind.'

'Spike,' cried Mops, 'that is a *brilliant* idea! I never knew you had it in you!'

And with that she put her hands round Filia's mouth so that she couldn't call for help – although, strangely, the bear cub hadn't even tried to. For his part, Benjamin dived at Filia's rear paws to hold them tight. Small as they were, her claws still looked horribly dangerous.

Only Armstrong had already picked up the vine-rope. With him at one end and Roger Broadback at the other, they quickly wound it round Filia's arms and legs. Satisfied that the knots were tight and that Bearon Weimar's daughter-cub couldn't even walk, let alone run away, Spike released his grip.

'Now listen, you,' he snarled in Filia's ear. 'Mops is going to take her hands away from your mouth. But don't even think about calling for help, 'cos if you do you'll find yourself in that sap-trap quicker than you can say, er...'

'Help?' suggested Mops.

And with that she slowly eased her fingers away from Filia's muzzle. The bear-cub's eyes darted this way and that, but she didn't open her mouth. Spike and Benjamin then picked her up – discovering with some surprise just how heavy even a small bear cub was – and laid her on her back. Only then did Filia say something.

'I agree with Mops,' she said. 'What a brilliant idea.'

'I... I don't understand,' said Benjamin, in disbelief. He'd expected a defiant screech of "help", or a furiously Mops-like, 'how dare you!' – but not what he'd just heard. 'You mean you *want* us to take you hostage?'

'Yes,' said Filia simply. 'I am sure your friend is correct. My father loves me. He will agree to anything to keep me safe – even if it means making you all safe too. Now you should find a strong branch you can use as a pole. But be quick. Petrifus will be wondering where I've got to.'

Roger Broadback quickly found just what they needed, a good, thick pole snapped from an overgrown nut-bush.

'Now slide it under the vine-rope you've tied me up with,' said Filia, still laying on her back. She waited until they'd done so, threading the pole through the rope from her shoulders down to her rear paws. 'Now you're going to have to pick me up and carry me. You'll probably need two of you at the front of the pole and two of you at the back.'

They did as she said, with Spike and Mops taking the front and Only and Roger the rear. Filia dangled helplessly from the pole, her head between Mops and Spike.

'Now, Benjamin,' said Filia. 'In this position all I can see are the tree tops. I am not going to know where you are taking me, so listen to this next part very carefully.'

'I'm listening,' said Benjamin, still unsure that he could believe what he was hearing.

'You must follow the path until you reach a shattered tree.' Filia gave Benjamin a grateful look. 'It was struck by lightning during that storm, just as I feared my tree was going to be.'

'Can we press on?' said Mops sharply.

'When you reach it,' continued Filia, 'do not follow the path any further. That will only bring you into the sap-hunter's main gathering-spot. It will also be the way that Petrifus comes if he returns to look for me. Instead, you must turn off the path and along a narrow track which you will see running through a grove of fir trees.'

'And where does that bring us?' asked Roger Broadback.

'To a *different* gathering-spot?' said Only Armstrong suspiciously.

Filia shook her head (as best as she was able, dangling upside down). 'It brings you almost to the edge of the magic-lake. There is a way from there across to the island in the centre. You should be able to reach it before any bear sees you.'

'Go over to an *island*?' snorted Mops. 'My dear cub, do you think we're stupid? We'd be walking straight into an even deadlier trap.'

'But that is exactly what you *must* do,' said Filia. 'Otherwise I cannot do the one thing that which will persuade my papa to let you go free.'

Benjamin frowned. 'And what's that?'

'Is it not obvious?' said Filia. 'I'm going to scream at him that unless he does what you want, you're going to throw me into the magic-lake to drown.'

THE MAGIC-LAKE

Bearon Weimar was feeling extremely irritable. Along with the other sap-hunters, he'd moved steadily through the long arm of the chasing-field which skirted the Hunting-Forest, fully expecting the hair-red either to be chased out into the open by the sap-scarers or to pop out from one of the tunnels connected to the sap-traps. Neither had happened. Other saps had appeared, to be hunted down with glee by his companions, but not the one special sap that Bearon Weimar was waiting for.

'Happened-what to hair-red-that?' he growled. 'The sap-scarers useless-are!' Then he remembered that his own daughter was amongst them and decided on a more precise target for blame. 'No! Petrifus too-far ancient-is!'

Beside him, Inspector Dictatum wasn't sure whether to be irritated or pleased. He, too, wasn't happy about the failure of the sap-scarers to flush out Benjamin Wildfire. It would happen sooner or later though. And when it did, wouldn't an annoyed Bearon Weimar be less likely to object to him tearing the hair-red to shreds 'accidentally'? That thought pleased him greatly.

So he simply said, 'Agree-me, Bearon Weimar. Have-Petrifus explaining-plenty when reach-we the gathering-spot.'

The gathering-spot was a large mound close to the furthermost point of the chasing-field. Beyond it, and reaching as far as the chasm, lay an impenetrable area of towering acorn-trees and vicious brambles. When the magic-lake had formed, its tentacles had extended way into this area too – leading the bears to name it 'the swamp-jungle'. Venturing into this swamp-jungle was thought to be so impossible that the sap-hunt had always ended when the hunters reached the gathering-spot mound. There they swapped grisly tales of who they'd hunted and how. Sap weights were announced and the bears would discover which amongst them would have the honour of hanging their trophy in Bearon Weimar's private hunting-lodge.

So when Bearon Weimar arrived at the gathering spot and announced, 'The sap-hunt unfinished-is. Saps-some still-are large-at!' His words were met with astonished gasps, then a grim silence. Never before had they reached the gathering-spot without every single sap having been hunted down.

It was then that Bearon Weimar caught sight of the unfortunate Petrifus, leading his band of yellow-sashed sap-scarers out from the Hunting-Forest.

'Explain-you, Petrifus!' roared Bearon Weimar at once, 'where-went the hair-red?'

'And friends-of-him?' growled Inspector Dictatum. 'Them-either seen-me-not.'

Before the old bear could answer either of these questions, Bearon Weimar was barking out another, even more angrily. 'And is-where daughter-mine? Leave-me-her in care-yours!'

Petrifus didn't know the answer to the first two questions, but this third one was a different matter. 'Filia tired-was, Bearon Weimar,' he said, bowing low. 'Said-she rest-let. Said-she up-would-catch.'

Bearon Weimar's voice rose even further. 'Left-you daughter-my alone-all?' he howled at the grovelling Petrifus, 'with saps loose-still? Me-you-with later-deal!'

Galloping to the top of the mound, he roared across the length and breadth of the gathering-spot, 'Daughter-mine lost-is! Form-you-all a party-search!'

The hunting-bears didn't need telling twice. Every one of them sprang to their paws. Cub-searching wasn't going to be anything like as satisfying as sap-shredding, but it promised to be rewarding in a different way: whichever of them was lucky enough to find Filia Weimar would be the bearon's friend for life.

'Scour-you Hunting-Forest from bottom-top!' roared Bearon Weimar, pointing deep into the trees to make sure that even the slowest thinker knew where he was talking about.

And so it was that, at the very moment Benjamin and the others peered out warily from the far corner of the Hunting-Forest, it was to find that every bear in the gathering-spot was looking the other way.

The route they'd followed had been exactly as Filia had described. Reaching the grove of fir-trees, they'd turned away from the main pathway and headed along the narrow track they'd found there. With Filia dangling from the pole between the others, Benjamin led the way.

'How far is it to the magic-lake?' he asked.

'Six-hundred and seventy-four paw-paces,' said Filia at once. She looked up at a surprised Benjamin. 'I like counting. I am not a bear with little brain.'

'I hope so, matey-bear,' said Spike, supporting the pole close to Filia's head, 'because if you're trying to trick us, you're going to find yourself in that magic-lake before you know what's happened.'

'I am not tricking you,' said Filia.

'Why do you call it the magic-lake?' asked Benjamin.

'Because it appeared like magic,' said Filia. 'That is what my papa says. Once it was just a small lake, an oval of two hundred paw-paces by one hundred, fed from the rocks and overflowing into the chasm. In those times it was possible to swim in the chasm. My papa's own papa had a flopping-board made for my papa to use. That is how it was for hunting-season after hunting-season...until they arrived one season to find that the chasm was almost dry, and a great lake – at least three hundred paw-paces by two hundred – had magically appeared.'

'There it is!' hissed Mops.

Having threaded their way between two spreading pines, the track had taken a sharp turn. Now, straight ahead, just as Filia had told them, the trees ended – and beyond it was a narrow strip of ground leading through the waters of the lake to a small island just about one hundred paw-paces away.

Gesturing the others to stop, Benjamin moved cautiously ahead. He peered out, at the very moment that Bearon Weimar – in the gathering-spot way out to their right – was attracting every hunting-bear's attention.

No more than a paw-pace wide, the strip of ground in front of Benjamin was slippery and muddy, as if it had itself recently been underwater. At that moment, he realised how the magic-lake might have come about. Something had caused the original lake to burst its banks and send water cascading down and out into a large, previously dry hollow. The strip of ground must have been part of the original bank. Nowadays it would be covered when rain made the lake rise or – as now – uncovered when it fell.

Benjamin urgently beckoned the others forward. They hurried up, still with Mops and Spike at the front of the carrying pole, Roger and Only Armstrong at the rear, and Filia suspended helplessly from the pole between them.

'Filia was telling the truth,' said Benjamin. 'There's the island.'

The island was speckled with weeping-trees, their long, thin branches trailing down into the lake. As for what lay behind the weeping-trees, that they would only discover when they got across to it. It was Spike who put their doubts into words.

'But if her plan don't work, we're trapped, ain't we? Those bears'll be able to come and get us, or leave us stuck there until we starve.'

'What choice do we have?' said Mops quietly.

'None, unless you trust me,' urged Filia, upside down. 'Now are you going, or not?'

Benjamin looked at the others. Slowly, Spike nodded. Then Mops. Then Roger Broadback and Only Armstrong.

'We're going,' said Benjamin decisively.

And with a deep breath he led them, slithering and sliding, on to the strip of ground leading across the magic-lake.

Petrifus, the sap-scarer's leader, was feeling mightily upset. It wasn't his fault that Filia Weimar had stayed behind to have a rest. It wasn't his fault that she hadn't caught up. He hadn't wanted to look after her in the first place. Now he was going to get into serious trouble, and all because of her.

At that moment there were a hundred things that Petrifus would like to growl-bellow loudly at Filia

Weimar if and when he saw her again. Not one of those hundred, however, included what he actually *did* growl-bellow as a sudden far-awat movement caught his eye.

'Stop-you! Filia there-is!'

The strip of ground was treacherously slippery but Benjamin found that he could move quickly if he kept to the driest part in the very centre. He yelled at the others behind him to do the same. With the job of carrying Filia on the bouncing pole without his help, they were having to watch their steps even more carefully. They'd got about halfway when Petrifus's growl-bellow resounded across the waters of the magic-lake like gunfire.

'What are we going to do?' shouted Spike.

Alerted by Petrifus, the hunting-bears had stopped running towards the forest and had turned back. Now, to Benjamin's horror, they were swarming towards the banks of the magic-lake.

'Keep going!' cried Filia. 'You must reach the island!'

And so they ran on, with Benjamin trying to watch where he was going while at the same time looking across the lake at what was happening on the banks. Three or four of the hunting-bears were already close to the water's edge. Any moment now they would be leaping in and swimming towards them…

But the island was getting closer. Benjamin could

clearly see the leaf-carpeted earth around the base of the weeping-trees. He gritted his teeth and tried not to think of the terrible punishment they'd all face if Filia's plan went wrong. On he went, until he found himself slithering the last few steps across the strip of ground and tumbling through the thin branches of the weeping-trees as if they were a curtain. Behind them lay a circle of bare earth, about ten paw-paces in size. Moments later, the others arrived. Gasping with both effort and fear, they laid Filia on the ground at once. Bearon Weimar's daughter-cub had been squealing loudly all the way across but now she stopped.

'Remove the pole!' she cried. 'Let me stand up!'

Spike shook his head. 'Not on your life, matey. Next you'll be wanting to be untied and then *next* you'll be leaping in that lake and swimming back for all you're worth.'

'Leaving us at your papa's mercy,' added Mops.

At that moment Bearon Weimar's voice carried loudly across the water – and it didn't sound in the least bit merciful.

'Saps-those have daughter-my! Lake-swim! Island-attack! Reward-huge for hunting-bear who Filia-saves!'

On the other side of the lake the leading bear plunged in to the water. Others began racing round towards the strip of ground leading to the island. It wouldn't take the swimming bears that long to plough the

182

hundred or so paw-paces to the island. They might even arrive before the runners, whose route around the lake's bank to the strip of ground had to be at least three hundred paw-paces. Either way, they didn't have long.

'Say your bit, Filia,' said Benjamin sharply. 'Now!'

Filia did just that.

True to her word, she screamed at the top of her voice. 'Papa! Send-not the hunting-bears! If-do-you, saps-these me-drown!'

For one brief moment there was no response, as if Bearon Weimar was thinking over what he'd just heard. Benjamin gave Spike the slightest nudge. In two short steps they'd carried Filia out through the weeping-tree branches to dangle her at the water's edge.

'Papa!' screamed Filia again. 'Not-them time-have to me-reach!'

That was when Bearon growl-roared again. 'Stop-you, hunting-bears-all! Command-me back-you-come!'

The running bears slithered to a halt. Slowly they turned back. In the water, the hunting-bears who'd been swimming towards the island began to manoeuvre themselves round in a large sweep and were soon paddling back to the bank.

Filia's ruse had worked.

They were safe – for now.

THE BARGAIN

An uneasy calm settled over the magic-lake and the gathering-spot, broken only by growl-shouts from Bearon Weimar and replies from Filia.

'Know-you-how saps-those drown-you-will?' shouted the Bearon.

'They-me-tell, Papa!' called Filia.

'*They*-you-tell? Mean-you saps-those *bear-talk*?'

'Yes, Papa. Saps-these bears-understand.'

Even from a distance away, Bearon Weimar's snort of disbelief could be heard. 'That impossible-is, Filia!'

'True-is, Papa! But more-there-is…' Filia braced herself. It was time to reveal her secret. 'Can-me human-talk!'

Now an even louder snort of disbelief – this time mixed with anger – carried across the lake. Benjamin knew it had come from Inspector Dictatum, even before that great evil bear's voice confirmed as much.

'It-prove!' he roared. 'Ask-you names-them!'

'Have-me it-proved already. Me-you-told Benjamin Wildfire here-was in place-first!'

There was a pause, as if Inspector Dictatum was thinking this over (which he was). In the fading light the bears on the far side of the lake were turning into dark shadows, but his massive outline was unmistakable. Then he roared once more.

'Again-it-prove! Ask-you-names of Wildfire friends-best!'

'Spike Brownberry,' said Spike.

'Millicent Ophelia Patience Snubnose,' snapped Mops. 'Mops for short.'

Filia called back immediately. 'Spike Brownberry and Millicent Ophelia Patience Snubnose!' A pause. 'Mops short-for!'

At this point, Benjamin gave Filia one more piece of information to call out across the lake. 'Them-you-know sure-for, Inspector. Say-them present-were-you when name-collars removed-were in Howling-Tower!'

'Proof-enough!' Bearon Weimar called. 'Believe-you-me!'

But Inspector Dictatum needed just a little more evidence. He bellowed out one last question. 'Ask-you hair-red for mother-name and father-name.'

Benjamin told Filia what they were – and more besides. 'Father-name is Duncan Wildfire. Papa, him-you-have up-locked.'

'True-is!' called a shocked Bearon Weimar. But this shock was as nothing compared to the bolt that struck him when Filia called out to him again.

'And mother-name is Alicia Wildfire. Papa, is-she the never-move won-you from King Antonius!'

'True-well-as!' howled Bearon Weimar, now utterly convinced.

Lady Weimar didn't approve of betting, so winning the never-move from King Antonius had been something he'd not mentioned at home. Filia could only have discovered that fact from the saps. Which meant that they *could* understand bears – and by some mysterious process that Bearon Weimar simply couldn't fathom, Filia could understand them. All of which meant that her claims that the saps would throw her in the lake to drown weren't mere suspicions – that *must* be what they'd told her.

A desperate, gnawing fear entered his stomach. For all his faults, Bearon Weimar was a parent and, like any parent, would do anything it took to save his dear cub from harm. Well, he thought…if the saps could say what they were *intending* to do, then they could also say what it would take to *stop* them doing it.

'Filia, daughter-my!' he roared across the lake. 'Want-what saps-those to free-you-set?'

'All of us to be allowed to leave here,' Benjamin reminded Filia, 'and my parents too.'

Filia shouted her reply. 'Hunt-them-not, Papa. Free-them. Free-also the Benjamin-father and Benjamin-mother.'

Hearing this, Bearon Weimar winced. To allow the

saps to go free was an irritation, but no more. There were plenty of saps to hunt where they'd come from. But allow the hair-red to go? And his father? And his mother? The family of hair-reds he was going to give to the new King Bruno to ensure that he was chosen as the next Chancellor? That needed more thought.

'Agree-you!' came a fierce growl in his ear.

The bearon turned to see Lady Weimar, her face like thunder. Normally a wife who gave the impression of being perfectly happy so long as she had plenty of rounds to spend (hence her objection to him losing it by betting), she had hot wet tears running down her snout. 'Forget-you-not also-Filia daughter-mine,' she said. 'Her-me into-shape-licked.'

Bearon Weimar hesitated. Mothers. They simply didn't understand what reputation was all about. This wasn't a simple decision. Bears got to positions such as his by strength and ruthlessness, not by showing weakness. Making the wrong decision could ruin him. Then another voice, in his other ear, offered exactly the same advice.

'Lady Weimar right-is, Bearon,' growled Inspector Dictatum. 'Must agree-you.' He added with a sincere look, 'Daughter-yours is important-most.'

Bearon Weimar sighed. If even a sap-hater like Inspector Dictatum thought that way then he had no choice but to give in. He would do as the saps wanted. 'Well-very,' he nodded, 'will-me them-take to den-my.

The Wildfire-parents released-will-be. Then off-go they-can.'

'No, no, no!' said Inspector Dictatum sharply, before quickly softening his tone. Very rarely had he ever had a quick thought, but one had miraculously come to him now. 'Suggest-me plan-another, Bearon. Go-me den-yours and back-bring the Wildfire-parents to Hide-Park.'

'For-what?'

'Think-me the Benjamin-sap will see-want parents-his before free-him daughter-yours,' said Inspector Dictatum smoothly.

Bearon Weimar scratched his chin thoughtfully. 'So-me-suppose.'

Inspector Dictatum gave him no time to change his mind. 'Then go-me once-at,' he said at once. 'Will back-me-be by sun-come!'

And before Bearon Weimar could say another word, the great bear was loping away from the gathering-spot.

On the island in the middle of the lake, Benjamin and the others were now told the news.

'Agree-me to demands-your!' they heard Bearon Weimar shout, 'the Wildfire-parents are brought-being. Arrive-they by sun-come. Safe-you-are then-until!'

Benjamin turned to the others in triumph. 'Hear that? My mother and father are on the way! We're all going to be saved!'

Spike and Mops, Roger Broadback and Only Armstrong, smiled broadly. Filia, feeling as though she'd started to make up for the part she'd played in the terrible events of the sap-hunt, smiled a smile of hope.

On the other side of the lake, Lady Weimar was smiling and drying her tears at the same time. Beside her, Bearon Weimar, who had suddenly realised that a daughter-cub who could speak to saps could be a very valuable daughter indeed, was smiling too.

But of all these, none was smiling more broadly than Inspector Dictatum. As his powerful legs began to eat up the ten thousand paw-paces to Bearon Weimar's den, he was already thinking about exactly what he was going to do when he brought Duncan and Alicia Wildfire back to Hide-Park to join their wretched son.

Oh, revenge was going to be sweet!

On the island nobody slept, neither human nor bear.

Spike and Mops were sitting beneath the weeping-tree nearest to where the strip of ground met the island. The light of a brilliant autumn moon enabled them to see clearly all the way across to where they themselves had emerged from the Hunting-Forest. They were keeping watch, just in case Bearon Weimar should break his word. As Spike had said grimly, 'It's not that I don't like it being all quiet like this, it's just that I want to be certain it's going to stay that way.'

On the other side of the tiny island, Roger Broadback and Only Armstrong were anxiously watching the gathering-spot. If any bears attempted to swim across, they'd see them at once.

As for Benjamin, he was guarding Filia. Although no longer attached to the carrying-pole, her front and rear paws were still securely tied together by the vine-rope.

'Do you not trust me,' sighed Filia, 'not even now?'

'I *do*...' said Benjamin slowly.

'You do not sound certain.'

Benjamin hesitated. He'd had a nagging feeling about Filia for some while now. Not so much a doubt, as a question mark.

'Why are you doing this?' he asked finally.

'I told you,' replied Filia. 'I am saving you, because you saved me.'

'You're doing more than that, Filia. You're risking your life. If this plan doesn't work, we could throw you in the lake to drown. Now – why?'

Filia shook her head. 'I do not know.' She corrected herself at once. 'No, what I mean is: I cannot explain it. The reason is inside me. When I helped chase the large sap out of the cabins, and even more when I heard the cries of the saps caught by the hunting-bears inside me I felt...unhappy.'

'That's because what you were doing was wrong,' said Benjamin angrily.'

'*Wrong*?' echoed Filia. 'What is *wrong*? We do not have this word in bear-language.'

'You do. I've heard it used lots of times.'

'Yes,' said Filia. 'Sums can be wrong. Choosing a root that makes you ill is wrong. But not *doing* wrong. Bears do what bears do. It is not right or wrong. It just is.'

'Well it shouldn't be. Bears should realise that things you *do* can be wrong as well!'

'I see,' said Filia thoughtfully – but she didn't say any more.

The silence suited Benjamin. It gave him time to look forward to the moment when he would see his mother and father again. What would they do after that, when Bearon Weimar freed them?

If Bearon Weimar freed them. Could Filia's father really be trusted to do that? Could any bear who was friendly with the evil Inspector Dictatum ever be fully trusted?

Benjamin didn't know. He could only hope for a better life in the future. But with his dreams of freedom in Hide-Park now cruelly shattered, would that life ever be more than an endless saga of running and hiding and fear? Even so, the thought of being reunited with his parents made Benjamin's heart sing.

So deep in thought was he that it came as a surprise when he noticed that sun-come had lifted

191

the darkness. Beyond the lake, the horizon was tinged with light blue. Benjamin looked quickly at Filia. She hadn't moved. Still curled up in a ball, her eyes were tightly closed.

Seeing that she had dropped off to sleep, Benjamin got to his feet. He wandered the dozen or so steps that it took to reach the other side of the island – that which was reached by crossing the strip of ground. And there, as the lightening sky allowed him to look down into the water, he saw that his theory about how the magic-lake had formed simply had to be correct. Another strip of ground, submerged by perhaps a finger's-depth of water, led away from this side of the island towards the impenetrable area the bears called swamp-jungle. He bent down and put his hand into the water, playing it back and forth over the slimy mud beneath. This slightly lower part had to be where the bank of the lake had continued.

Benjamin stood up again and gazed across to the rock wall, not so far away. All dark-time he'd been able to hear the sound of cascading water. Now he could see it, coursing down hidden crevices in the rock wall before falling over a narrow ledge and down into the lake below. There the water swirled and eddied around a number of large trees that must have crashed down into the lake at some time in the past.

So why had the lake overflowed its banks and become far bigger? And hadn't Filia said that the chasm, once filled with water, had run dry at the same time? How could that have happened too?

As Benjamin stared across at the fallen trees, the explanation came to him in a flash. Like a cork in a bottle, those trees had to be stopping the water from reaching the chasm! The overflow point had to be beyond them – and he could almost certainly see where that point was. Between the spot at which the rock wall ended and the furthermost point of the swamp-jungle began, there was a smallish gap, ten paces wide at the most. If the fallen trees had blocked that, the rising waters would have had nowhere else to go but to wash over the lower banks and form the magic-lake...

'Benjamin!'

Roger Broadback's hiss abruptly interrupted Benjamin's thoughts. He hurried back past the stirring Filia, to join Roger and Only Armstrong at their watching place opposite the gathering-spot. Mops and Spike scurried across from their posts near the strip of ground.

'What is it?' asked Benjamin.

Roger simply pointed. Outlined against the pink-tinged sky was the silhouette of a bear so massive that it could only be Inspector Dictatum, tramping across the chasing-field as he headed for the gathering-spot. Either side of him were two humans. Dwarfed by the great bear, they looked like a couple of children – but Benjamin knew they weren't. He felt a surge of joy, mingled with fear.

His parents were here. The three of them were going to survive together...or perish together.

CROSS-DOUBLE

The figures gradually took shape. The towering outline of Inspector Dictatum drew close enough for Benjamin to see his fur shimmer in the light as he stalked towards the gathering-spot. On each side of the great bear, and attached to him by ropes or chains, struggled Duncan and Alicia Wildfire.

Benjamin only had the briefest glimpse of his parents before they disappeared into the throng of hunting-bears awaiting their arrival – but it was enough. His spirits soared. He felt strong enough to fight any bear and win. So when his parents didn't immediately re-emerge, he swung round on Filia, his fists clenched.

'What's going on?' he cried. 'Tell me!'

Filia answered with a question of her own. 'Do you trust my papa?'

'Not likely,' interjected Spike.

'No offence,' said Mops, 'but in our experience trustworthy bears have been rather thin on the ground.'

Filia didn't look surprised. 'Which is why I suspect that my papa is now working out how to make the exchange in a way that will satisfy you – but not put me in any danger.'

And so it proved. After a little more delay, during which the silvery-grey figure of Bearon Weimar was seen talking urgently and receiving nods from all around, the crowd of bears parted. Through them stepped Bearon and Lady Weimar. They were followed by Inspector Dictatum, and Duncan and Alicia Wildfire.

Fuelled by his thoughts of revenge, Inspector Dictatum had dragged them all the way from Bearon Weimar's den in a small cage-cart all by himself. Before releasing them for the march to the gathering-spot, the powerful bear had chained Duncan Wildfire to his left side and Alicia Wildfire to his right. The ends to both these chains were looped around his neck and secured by a padlock. The key to this padlock was clamped securely between his teeth.

'Filia, daughter-my,' Bearon Weimar now boomed across the lake. 'Me-show well-you-are.'

Filia was helped to the edge of the island by Roger Broadback and Only Armstrong. 'Well-me-am, Papa!'

'Then tell-you saps-those now-what happen-will.'

'Need-me-not,' called Filia. 'Them-understand bear-speak, remember-you?'

Bearon Weimar *had* remembered. It was just that he still found it so difficult to believe. Saps didn't think. They didn't talk sensibly. They simply weren't *bear*-like.

'Well-very,' he shouted again. 'Is-this what happen-will. Bring-we-shall the hair-red grown-olders to ground-strip. Then to-island walk-them. At time-same, release-you Filia so walk-she us-to.'

'That leaves us all trapped here!' said Mops. Her objections, though, were immediately dealt with by Bearon Weimar.

'When have-we Filia, leave-us Hide-Park. Promise-me return-we-not until season-next. By-then saps-those must gone-be...else-or!'

'How do we know we can trust them?' asked Roger Broadback.

'They could still attack us,' said Only Armstrong.

'Once a bear, always a bear,' said Spike grimly.

Benjamin turned to Filia. 'Can we trust your papa to do what he says?'

Filia looked uncertain. 'I do not know. But you can trust me.' She called out across the lake once more. 'Promise-me attack-you-not swap-after, Papa!'

Bearon Weimar boomed back. 'Have-me-that ready-all promised-them.'

'Not promise-them, Papa,' Filia cried. 'Promise-*me*!'

There was a pause, as if Bearon Weimar had just had one final devious thought swept from his mind. Finally he growl-called. 'Well-very. Daughter-my. *You*-me-promise...'

Filia turned to Benjamin. 'Papa has *never* broken a promise to me. You may not trust him – but *I* do.'

Benjamin looked at the others. They were all nodding. Spike put it into words in his own unique way: 'I *don't* don't like it, matey!'

'Which means he likes it,' sighed Mops. 'I think.'

Filia was in no doubt. 'Agree-they, Papa!' she shouted across the lake. 'Ready-getting am-me!'

Gazing intently from his side of the water, Bearon Weimar saw his daughter being untied by the saps. He saw them lead her to the edge of the island, to the point where the strip of firm ground met it, and stopped. It was what he'd wanted to see.

'Them-unchain,' he said to Inspector Dictatum.

The great bear's eyes flickered. His mouth opened – but only to let the key he was holding between his ugly yellow teeth fall into a sharp-clawed paw. Deftly he used it to undo the chains holding Duncan and Alicia Wildfire fast. Then he stepped back.

'Me-you-want them-take, Bearon?' he asked.

Bearon Weimar shook his head. 'No. Nor them-me-take. Want-me saps-those trust-thinking. The hair-red grown-olders alone-go.'

Inspector Dictatum felt a flash of irritation. He had a plan, but would prefer not to use it unless it was completely necessary. Catching the Benjamin hair-reds would be so much easier if he already had the parents in his claws.

'Know-me Wildfire-saps, Bearon!' he urged.

'Trust-them-not! Them-leave me-with!'

But again Bearon Weimar refused. 'Here-you-stay, Inspector!' he barked. 'Go-them-alone!'

And with that, the bearon nudged Duncan and Alicia away from the gathering-spot mound and out towards the lake. They walked unsteadily forward, looking behind them to see if they were being followed. But by the time they'd reached the lakeside, those fears had begun to subside. Not a bear was following them. Duncan gripped his wife's hand. Alicia gave him a smile of hope. Hand-in-hand they began to walk more quickly, following the curving bank of the magic-lake towards the ground-strip in the distance.

Inspector Dictatum watched them go. He stayed, as ordered, his evil eyes glinting as he watched two of the three saps he hated most in the world walking away from his clutches. He stayed like this until Duncan and Alicia Wildfire were about half-way towards their destination. Then, unnoticed by Bearon Weimar, he gradually began to edge away from the gathering-spot mound and towards the tangled morass of the swamp-jungle. A burning rage filled his heart – a rage so powerful that nothing, not even needle-sharp thorns and sucking mud, would be able to hold him back. Within moments he was clawing and splashing a path through the swamp-jungle towards the side of the island from which none of the saps would be expecting danger to emerge.

Benjamin had been standing, with Filia beside him, watching his parents' long walk round the lake. Now, as they finally reached the far end of the ground-strip, Filia turned to him.

'Your parents are here, Benjamin,' said the young cub. 'Now I must go to mine.'

Benjamin smiled and nodded. 'Thank you for everything, Filia Weimar.'

Filia shook her head. 'No – thank *you*, Benjamin Wildfire.'

She began to pad slowly along the ground-strip. At the same moment, Duncan and Alicia Wildfire began their walk towards the island – Alicia ahead and Duncan following. But as Filia met them in the middle of the ground-strip, all three of them stopped. The strip was too narrow for them to squeeze by each other.

It was Filia who rescued the awkwardness of the moment. With a laugh she turned to the side and dived into the water. 'Quicker for me to swim!' she cried, then struck out towards Bearon and Lady Weimar, waiting and waving at the side of the lake near the gathering-spot.

Slowly – oh, so slowly it seemed to Benjamin – his parents continued walking towards him. And then they were there, on the island, hugging him and wiping away their tears of joy.

That was when Inspector Dictatum struck.

Wading out from the swamp-jungle, he let loose a howl of rage. Blood and ragged bits of bramble clung to his fur. Filthy water lapped up to his belly, hiding his legs from view – until, rising upright, 'Hate-me hair-reds!' he bellowed.

Just a narrow stretch of water was separating him from them. He could clearly see the father, Duncan, who'd first escaped from him in the Howling-Tower; the mother, Alicia, sold by him to King Antonius; and, finally, Benjamin Wildfire, the sap who'd led the break-out from the Howling-Tower and who'd caused him to lose his job. He hated them, all three of them, and now he was going to wreak a terrible revenge.

As he launched himself full length and began to thrash his way through the water towards the tiny island, there was only one question swirling through Inspector Dictatum's mind: which of the three would he rip to pieces first?

Hearing the evil bear's angry bellow, Benjamin broke away from his father and mother.

'Run!' he cried. 'Back across the ground-strip!'

For a moment, nobody moved. Mops wailed in fear. Spike, Roger and Only Armstrong seemed rooted to the spot. Even Benjamin's parents looked as though they didn't know what to do, so sudden and terrifying had Inspector Dictatum's emergence from the swamp-jungle been.

'Lead them, Father!' screamed Benjamin. 'Quickly! I'll follow!'

Duncan Wildfire reacted at once. Clutching Alicia by the hand, he began to run back along the ground-strip towards the trees of the Hunting-Forest at the far end. Stung into action, Mops and Spike followed, then Roger Broadback and Only Armstrong.

It wasn't until they reached the end of the ground-strip that they realised Benjamin hadn't followed them...

Filia had swum no more than halfway across to where Bearon and Lady Weimar were waiting when she heard Inspector Dictatum's howl of rage. By the time she'd begun to tread water to see what was happening, the great bear was already thrashing his way towards the island.

'Papa!' cried Filia bitterly, 'Me-you-promised safe-they-be!'

'Not-me Dictatum-send!' growl-shouted Bearon Weimar. 'Guilty-him of cross-double!'

But Filia didn't hear this. She'd already turned back towards the island and was swimming as fast as she could.

Benjamin *had* heard Bearon Weimar's growl-shout. So Inspector Dictatum wasn't acting on the bearon's orders, but out of revenge! Surely that meant the bearon and his hunting-bears would protect the others if they could get across the ground-strip and away. *If* they could get away...

Inspector Dictatum would have to be slowed down, realised Benjamin, or made to change direction. *That* was it. If he could decoy him away from the ground-strip it would buy the others the time they needed. He'd fooled the stupid, evil bear before. Could he do it again?

Yes, he could! Remembering something he'd discovered a little earlier gave Benjamin an idea of how it could be done.

He raced the few steps it took to reach the other side of the island, and saw again the submerged ground that must have been the bank of the lake before it had overflowed. Looking further out to where the huge fallen tree lay in the water, he could see that some of its roots were still embedded in a raised mound of dry earth. The conclusion was obvious. The raised mound must also have been part of the original bank – which meant that the submerged ground had to lead all the way there!

Taking a deep breath, Benjamin stepped out into the waters of the magic-lake...and began to walk.

The sight of the hair-red appearing to walk on water greatly confused Inspector Dictatum. But it didn't slow him down – for, as he thrashed his way closer to the island, he suddenly found the huge claws of his rear paws beginning to dig into the bed of the lake.

His dull brain worked quickly for once. The water was getting shallower. The spot where the sap was walking could only be a claw's length deep. The great bear felt a surge of delight. The fool had played right into his paws. As the one who'd cost him his job and his reputation, the Benjamin-sap was the one he wanted first. And when the Duncan-sap and Alicia-sap saw him go for their son they would stop running away. Quite the opposite. In fact Inspector Dictatum was sure that they would run back and try their feeble best to save their beloved son. He wouldn't need to chase after them. *They* would come to *him*!

And so, scrambling up the final short distance to the island, Inspector Dictatum didn't hesitate. In a cloud of spray and mud he began to lumber along the submerged bank after Benjamin – until, ahead of him, he saw the hated sap give a sudden lurch to one side…and topple into the lake.

Never having learned how to swim, Benjamin had had to choose his moment carefully. What had looked to Inspector Dictatum like a topple had, to Benjamin, been a heart-stopping dive. He wanted to reach the top part of the fallen tree's trunk, some way out into the lake, and there had been only one way he could see of managing that without swimming. The weed-covered branches of the tree were spread in all directions. Some jutted through the gap where the waters of the lake had once flowed to dangle dangerously over the chasm. Others were jammed against the side of the gap itself. Most importantly, many more were protruding from the water not too far from the submerged bank. It was these that Benjamin had deliberately dived towards.

What he had to do now was make it as difficult as possible for Inspector Dictatum to catch hold of him. And he'd anticipated a way in which that would be possible. The half-sunken branches, even with the clutter of dead wood and weeds pressing behind them, hadn't been totally squashed together. He could see a watery gap further in from where he was. Sucking one great breath of air into his lungs, Benjamin dived beneath the water.

He came up in the perfect position. Not only was he now protected by a circle of branches, Inspector Dictatum – he hoped – would have trouble seeing him at all.

This was indeed the case. The great bear had followed Benjamin in diving back into the lake. He'd been almost within touching distance when he'd seen the accursed sap disappear beneath the surface of the water. Now, as he reached the outer branches of the fallen tree, he could see no sign of him. Angrily he swam back and forth, peering into the tangle.

Then he saw the one thing that Benjamin was unable to hide – the one thing about him that would always stand out starkly against a background of green and brown: his red hair.

'You-got!' snarled Inspector Dictatum.

But it wasn't quite as simple as that. As he lunged a vicious claw in Benjamin's direction, the tangle of dead branches got in his way. He pulled himself free and tried again. Once more he found himself entangled. There was only one thing to do. Snarling angrily, the great bear began to rip away the branches that stood between him and the sap he now wanted to rip apart more than anything in Bear Kingdom.

Suddenly, he felt a sharp pain in the side of his neck. And heard a cry, 'Stop-you! Stop-you!'

It was Filia Weimar. She'd made it back to the island a good few counts after Inspector Dictatum had chased Benjamin along the submerged bank. She'd promptly followed them, though with little hope that she'd be in time to help Benjamin in any way at all. But the delays forced on Inspector Dictatum, firstly in searching for Benjamin, then trying to grab him, and finally in tearing away the floating branches, had allowed her to get within striking distance of the evil bear.

'Stop-you!' she cried again, digging her claws even deeper in to the side of Inspector Dictatum's neck.

With an angry roar, Inspector Dictatum lashed out. Caught by his heavy forearm, Filia let go of his neck. But she was still within range. Once again the enraged bear lashed out. This time he caught her full on the side of the head. With a low moan, Filia Weimar fell back into the water.

Benjamin had not seen this. He'd heard Filia's cries, of course, and been very grateful for her brave intervention. It had given him some breathing space in which to continue with his plan.

Pulling himself closer to the tree's massive trunk, he got a firm grip then hauled himself out of the water and on to the trunk's slimy green surface. Benjamin gasped. Although he'd been expecting it, the sight that greeted him was still very frightening. On the other side of the trunk, the chasm yawned. Just as he thought, the tree *was* stopping the water reaching it. No more than a few trickles were dribbling over the edge of the gap and down. Taking a deep breath, he hurried along the thick trunk as fast as he could. Once he reached the dry bank at the trunk's roots he could finish off what had always been his plan: to get Inspector Dictatum entangled in the branches of the fallen tree. Then he would run along its trunk to the dry mound and from there race back along the submerged bank to the island, the ground-strip and safety.

Two things stopped him.

Firstly, he saw Filia snout-up in the water. Eyes closed, her head was being propped up by a partly-submerged branch. After what she'd done, how could he leave her?

And the second thing was that, as he moved quickly along the tree trunk, it began to *move*.

To start with, the movement was so slight that Benjamin thought it was his imagination. But the closer he got to the trunk's torn roots the more his doubts disappeared. Even beneath his light weight, the massive trunk was *rocking*. And with every hasty step the rocking was getting stronger. Beneath the trunk the water was giving sudden little spurts. Now a new idea started to form.

In the Howling-Tower he'd tricked Inspector Dictatum into following him on to a branch that was too heavy to support him. Could the great bear be so stupid as to fall for the same trick again? Benjamin looked back. Having clawed aside the remaining branches Inspector Dictatum was hauling himself out of the water and up onto the fallen trunk.

Benjamin waited.

Blind with rage, Inspector Dictatum began to run towards him. And, as he got closer, the tree trunk rocked – slowly, then more and more, until with a sudden crack the trunk lurched sideways. Grunting with effort, Inspector Dictatum dug his great claws into its bark. The trunk lurched a little further – then stopped. He shot a look of pure menace at Benjamin.

'Luck-bad, hair-red,' he growled. 'Time-this shred-me-you.'

Benjamin turned, panic-stricken. His plan was in ruins. There was no way now that he could reach safety. All he could do was run to the very end of the trunk, to the dry bank, where what remained of the huge tree's roots were still embedded in the earth.

Correction – root.

As he landed on the dry bank and into the surprisingly shallow hole from which the tree had once grown, Benjamin saw that all but one of its roots must have been unearthed when the tree had crashed down. That was why the tree had rocked as he ran across it. Just one thick root was all that was keeping the tree anchored and preventing it from being swept away by the great weight of water pressing behind it.

Inspector Dictatum was almost on him.

So Benjamin cowered in the hole, bending his head

against this surviving root as if he was meekly waiting for the end.

It was the moment Inspector Dictatum had waited for. Dreamed about. The accursed hair-red was at his mercy…and mercy was not a word he had ever used.

He unsheathed his claws to their fullest. He drew back his strong, right paw. And then, taking careful aim, he lunged with all his might at the hair-red's slender neck.

Benjamin judged the moment to perfection. As he jerked his head away, Inspector Dictatum's massive claws sailed past and embedded themselves in the thick tree root against which he'd deliberately rested it.

The great bear howled in frustration. He pulled. He yanked. And, with a final piercing snap, the root gave way.

Now the fallen tree did more than rock. With the anchor of its last root snapped, the weight of the water pressing against the trunk was enough to make it move. The bottom part began to turn. Already close to the chasm, it now shifted enough to be pushed through the gap and dangle over the yawning drop. And still astride the bottom part of the tree trunk as he struggled to free his claws, was Inspector Dictatum.

With one final, desperate effort he tore his claws

away. He then quickly steadied himself, ready to leap from the trunk to safety. But the water was growing in strength with every moment, flowing powerfully through the gap he'd accidentally opened up and down into the chasm. Worse, the flow of water was now *lifting* the trunk. And the more it lifted, the more it rocked and swayed. Inspector Dictatum found himself losing his balance. Panic-stricken, he buried his fearsome claws deep into the bark of the bucking tree trunk and tried to hang on with every morsel of strength he could muster.

It was the worst – and final – decision of his life. At just that moment the torrent flowing into the chasm became powerful enough to carry the fallen tree that little bit further through the gap. Realising what was about to happen, Inspector Dictatum frantically tried to pull himself free. But he couldn't. With a great splintering of branches and shooting of spray, the fallen tree was swept down into the chasm, taking the evil bear with it.

From the far end of the ground-strip, where they'd stopped as soon as they'd realised that Benjamin hadn't followed them, a whooping and a hollering of delight came from Duncan and Alicia, Mops and Spike, Roger Broadback and Only Armstrong. Until that moment they'd been rooted to the spot with the horror and fear of it all. Now, still cheering wildly, they began to rush back across the ground-strip towards the island.

But Benjamin had no time to rejoice – for he could see what the others couldn't. In the water, still stunned from Inspector Dictatum's blow, was Filia Weimar.

She was being swept towards the gap.

FREEDOM

Benjamin thought frantically. There was no point in jumping in himself. That would be madness. He would be swept through the gap and down into the chasm in no time.

Filia was being swept closer – both to the gap *and* towards the dry bank where he was. The branch that had been supporting her head was still there. It was shaped like a letter Y, and Filia was stuck in the angle. Any moment now the long part of the branch would be close enough for him to reach out and touch.

Lying full-length, Benjamin stretched his arms out over the edge of the bank. He knew he would have just one chance of saving Filia. He mustn't fail.

Twisting and turning in the water, the branch was swept closer. Tensing himself for the effort, Benjamin thrust out his hands and grabbed it. The branch was slippery, but rough. The unconscious Filia was being buffeted by the swirling water. He had to get her out before she was washed out from the crook of the branch and over the gap. Gritting his teeth, he tried to pull the branch closer to him.

But it was no use. He simply wasn't strong enough. The power of the rushing water was making it impossible for him to do any more than hang on. What's more, Filia was regaining consciousness. Benjamin saw the confused panic suddenly flood into her eyes...

'Me-save!' he heard her scream.

As Filia began to struggle, Benjamin felt his strength fading fast. Any moment now he would either have to let the branch go – and Filia with it – or allow himself to be pulled from the dry bank and into the water himself.

Then, suddenly, a pair of paws had joined his hands around the end of the branch; a pair of paws, one of which had a claw missing.

'Me-do!' roared Bearon Weimar. 'Me-do!'

The silver-grey bear, who had dived into the lake to pursue Filia when he'd seen his daughter-cub swim back to confront Inspector Dictatum, hauled powerfully on the branch. In an instant, Filia was within reach. Letting the branch go, Bearon Weimar now reached out his four-clawed paw and grabbed her by the scruff of the neck. Moments later – as the branch plummeted over the gap and down into the chasm – she was safe on the dry bank.

Benjamin slumped back in relief. Bearon Weimar was relieved, too – but angry as well. 'Thought-me you-lost Filia,' he said, scooping his daughter-cub into his arms. 'What-doing, think-you?'

'Helping friend-my, Papa,' replied Filia.

'Friend-your?' echoed Bearon Weimar. He looked bleakly at Benjamin, then back to his daughter-cub. 'Sap-him. More-no, less-no.'

Filia shook her wet head vigorously. 'No, Papa. Wrong-you!'

Bearon Weimar's eyes narrowed. He gave a low growl, but said nothing in reply.

Beside them the water continued to pound down into the chasm, returning things to the way they'd looked many years before. The lake was already showing signs of returning to its original size. The submerged bank that Benjamin had discovered was submerged no longer. Sufficient water had already tumbled into the chasm to reveal a thin ribbon of mud arcing round to the island. Hoisting both Filia and Benjamin onto his back, Bearon Weimar began to pad slowly along it.

On the way, Filia told Bearon Weimar just a little of what she'd learned from Benjamin about the cruel things that bears did to humans. She also told him why she'd decided it was wrong.

Every so often Bearon Weimar nodded and said, 'Now-see-me, Filia. Never-before about-it-thought.'

'And not-them stupid-saps,' said Filia sharply as they reached the island. 'Are-them clever-saps. Clever-more bears-than!'

Bearon Weimar's eyes narrowed again. And again he

said nothing.

On the tiny island, growing larger by the moment as the water surrounding it receded, all was now joy. The moment Benjamin leapt from Bearon Weimar's broad back, he fell in to the arms of his parents. Through tears of happiness he introduced Filia and told them as much as he could about what had happened to bring them here.

'I am so proud of you,' said his mother, Alicia.

'So am I,' said Duncan, his father. 'More proud than I can say.'

'We all are,' said Mops.

'Definitely, matey,' said Spike.

Roger Broadback and Only Armstrong nodded wildly in agreement.

'That was the bravest thing I've ever seen,' said Mops. She smiled, and pulled back the collar of Benjamin's saturated shirt to give Spike a good view. 'And this is the cleanest neck I've ever seen!'

Their laughter was interrupted by the sound of Bearon Weimar's voice booming across to them. While the celebrations had been going on he'd hurried across the ground-strip and loped as quickly as he could round to where Lady Weimar and the rest of the hunting-party were still waiting at the gathering-spot. There, the silver-grey bear had gone straight to his tree-stump. Standing upright, his chain of office glinting, the bearon was now addressing the crowd.

'Hear-me! Decide-me again-never to sap-hunt!'

The hunting-party began to murmur, but Bearon Weimar silenced them angrily.

'Argue-not! More-is-what, make-me Hide-Park a sap-refuge. Saved-they daughter-my. Now-me them-save. From forth-hence, will-they here-live and free-run!'

Hearing this, Benjamin thought his heart would burst. Everything he'd ever hoped for had come to pass. In that moment, words almost failed him. All he could do was turn to Filia and say, 'Thank you, Filia Weimar.'

The bear cub shook her proud head. 'No. Thank *you*, Benjamin Wildfire.'

Bearon Weimar was as good as his word.

The hunting-party left, never to return. From that day on the only bear-visitors to Hide-Park were those bringing food to fill the hoppers – and eventually even they stopped coming as Benjamin and the others began to use the rich land of Hide-Park to grow their own food.

Slowly their community grew. Instead of buying saps to hunt, Bearon Weimar bought them to save. Every so often a boy or girl or grown-older man or woman would be ushered across the restored bridge to the one place where they could live in freedom.

That's not to say that all was perfect throughout Bear Kingdom, of course. There were still many places where saps remained at the mercy of their owners, still many bears who would mistreat them.

But, by the time that Filia Weimar became the first-ever she-bearon, things *had* begun to change. She continued the work her papa had begun, and more. She told her story to every bear she met. She tried to persuade them that saps had as much right to live in peace as bears did.

Like all grown-older bears, Filia slowly forgot how to speak human. But by then it had ceased to matter. Other special bear-cubs had discovered that they, too, had the same ability. And inspired by Filia's story they started to use a new word.

It was one of the few separate words in bear-language. Its meaning was: 'Being kind or merciful, and helping others without thinking about the cost to yourself.'

The word?

Human.

END OF VOLUME 3

DON'T MISS THE FIRST TWO VOLUMES
IN THE BEAR KINGDOM TRILOGY:

THE
HOWLING
TOWER

ISBN: 978 1 84362 938 2

AND

THE
FIGHTING
PIT

ISBN: 978 1 84616 214 5

Also by Michael Coleman

978 1 84362 183 6   £4.99

'You scared Daniel?'

How many times has Tozer said that to me? Hundreds.

But this time it's different. We're not in school. He hasn't got me in a headlock, with one of his powerful fists wrenching my arm up, asking 'You scared, Weirdo?'

No. We're here, trapped underground together with no way out.

Shortlisted for the *Carnegie Medal, Lancashire Children's Book Award* and *Writers Guild Award.*

'Tense and psychological.' *The Times*

978 1 84362 299 4   £4.99

Luke is a thief who knows that crime *does* pay. Besides, what other way is there for someone like him?

Then he meets Jodi. She might be blind, but she can see where Luke's life is going wrong. And she has a burning ambition that only Luke can help her fulfil...if she can trust him.

So Luke decides to go straight. But when old acquaintances want to use his talents for one last job, can he resist? Or will he end up on the run again?

More Orchard Books

The Fire Within	Chris d'Lacey	978 1 84121 533 4	£5.99
Icefire	Chris d'Lacey	978 1 84362 134 8	£5.99
Fire Star	Chris d'Lacey	978 1 84362 522 3	£5.99
The Snog Log	Michael Coleman	978 1 84121 161 9	£4.99
Tag	Michael Coleman	978 1 84362 182 9	£4.99
The Poltergoose	Michael Lawrence	978 1 86039 836 0	£4.99
The Killer Underpants	Michael Lawrence	978 1 84121 713 0	£5.99
The Toilet of Doom	Michael Lawrence	978 1 84121 752 9	£5.99
43 Bin Street	Livi Michael	978 1 84362 725 8	£4.99
Do Not Read This Book	Pat Moon	978 1 84121 435 1	£4.99
Do Not Read Any Further	Pat Moon	978 1 84121 456 6	£4.99
Do Not Read Or Else	Pat Moon	978 1 84616 082 0	£4.99
The Secret Life of Jamie B, Superspy	Ceri Worman	978 1 84362 389 2	£4.99
The Secret Life of Jamie B, Rapstar	Ceri Worman	978 1 84362 390 8	£4.99
The Secret Life of Jamie B, hero.com	Ceri Worman	978 1 84362 946 7	£4.99

Orchard Books are available from all good bookshops, or can be ordered direct
from the publisher: Orchard Books, PO BOX 29, Douglas IM99 1BQ
Credit card orders please telephone 01624 836000
or fax 01624 837033 or visit our Internet site: www.wattspub.co.uk
or e-mail: bookshop@enterprise.net for details.

To order please quote title, author and ISBN
and your full name and address.
Cheques and postal orders should be made payable to 'Bookpost plc.'
Postage and packing is FREE within the UK
(overseas customers should add £1.00 per book).

Prices and availability are subject to change.